Dancing With the Preying Mantis

By: R. Copperhead Scott

Order this book online at www.trafford.com
or email orders@trafford.com

Most Trafford titles are also available at major online book retailers.

Printed in Victoria, BC, Canada.

ISBN: 978-1-4269-1955-8 (sc)
ISBN: 978-1-4269-1954-1 (hc)

Library of Congress Control Number: 2009913517

*Our mission is to efficiently provide the world's finest, most comprehensive book publishing
service, enabling every author to experience success. To find out how to publish your book, your
way, and have it available worldwide, visit us online at www.trafford.com*

Trafford rev. 2/17/10

 www.trafford.com

North America & international
toll-free: 1 888 232 4444 (USA & Canada)
phone: 250 383 6864 ♦ fax: 812 355 4082

DEDICATION

To my loved ones who passed before their time Joshua Anthony (son) thirteen days, Mark Joseph (brother) thirty-two years Mary Ann (wife) fifty years and Carol Ann (mother) fifty-nine years gone but not forgotten.

About the author:

I was born and raised in Wheeling, West Virginia. I joined the WV Army National Guard (retired) attended West Virginia Northern Virginia Northern Community College and received an associate's degree in criminal justice. I moved to Washington DC and begin a career in security for the federal government. I achieved my goal of becoming a police officer in the Commonwealth of Virginia. I moved to Richmond, Virginia and would drive to northern Virginia for work. I'd listen to books on tape and CD from some of the great writers of today during the two hour journey. I was listening to an interview with an author who made the statement that she believed everyone had at least one good book in them. Her statement and the support of my family and friends made an impact and gave me the incentive to write the book that had been in my head for three years.

From *Webster's dictionary:*

Mantis: Etymology New Latin, from Greek, literally, diviner, prophet.

Definition: Any of a group of large insect-eating insects that hold their prey in their forelimbs as held in prayer.

What interests us here is the mating ritual of the mantis. According to the shows the nature channels air, the male of the species appears to hypnotize the female into a false sense of security before he mounts her to procreate. When the male is near the point of fertilizing her, she turns bites his head off and eats it. The narrator suggests that this may increase the chances of the female being fertilized.

Don't lose your head over a piece of tail.

PROLOGUE

She is awake but groggy. Her eyes are blurry and sandy with sleep. She feels cold and can not move. She thinks, *Were am I? How did I get here? Why am I so cold?* She can barely feel the goose bumps on her arm. Why is the rest of her body so cold? *Why I can't move my body,* she wonders. She only can roll her eyes. It is night, and she can see the stars in the sky and a full moon. It feels gritty on her back and butt. She realizes she is lying on sand, naked. Her body feels sticky, and it is so dammed cold. *I hope no insects or animals are attracted to this sticky substance on me.* She can't move no matter how hard she tries. She tries to call for help, but nothing comes from her mouth except mucus as she coughs.

Her mind starts to drift back into the abyss. She hears footsteps. "I am alive," she tries to shout but nothing comes out. A dark, shadowy figure appears over her and covers her body. The figure disappears into the night. She could not make out a face but wonders why the person did not help her. She is glad for the cover as she lapses into darkness.

CHAPTER 1:
THE INSURANCE SALESMAN

Upshur Logan couldn't complain. He'd enjoyed fairly good life. He enjoyed a football scholarship at Ohio State University after leaving that small town in the Kanawha Valley of West Virginia. He'd even gotten a ring from one of the bowl games the team played in and had been drafted in the late rounds to the pros. Everything had been going well until he'd blown his knee out in his sixth year for the third time ending his career. His wife had left him and taken the children. She'd found another pro athlete to marry. Now he got to see the kids once a month and sends a support check every two weeks. Logan was an average-looking man and had started to develop a small paunch belly. He was still in fairly good shape. He hadn't looked for another woman since his wife had left.

Logan had a friend from college George Hampshire who invited him to join the family insurance firm. George had run the firm since finishing college. Upshur took the job and rose to a vice president position quickly. The job included a lot of travel, which helped take his mind off some of his other problems. Upshur figured the money wasn't bad though it was nowhere near his pro salary. Luckily, he'd enough time in to collect a pension.

Logan had to go to the Washington, DC, area this week to conduct a presentation on medical insurance for a large company. The Hampshire Insurance Company was trying to venture into new products and the company needed Logan to set the tone for the new line. Logan arrived at the Goldberg Hotel in Arlington, Virginia on Sunday. He figured that the presentation wasn't until Wednesday in Reston, Virginia and he had several claims to settle in the area for the insurance company. He would have a little rest and could complete his work without too much stress. He settled in and went to the hotel restaurant. He needed to see the first client with the insurance pay out in the morning to settle that business. He could then take in some of the capitals sights. He had his laptop in the restaurant and was still working on the health insurance presentation.

The restaurant had mood lighting that was dim. Logan did not notice her entrance. Everyone else did. The light skinned woman entered the room, and it was as if it was a time warp had stopped everything. The cacophony in the bar seemed to stop if only for a second, when she walked into the room. The woman five foot nine inches with the face of an angel, and the build of a brick shithouse was of mixed race with light cinnamon skin. Her hair was shoulder length, and she wore sunglasses. She was dressed in a skirt of mint green with a slit up the thigh, a matching jacket, gloves that came to her elbows and an off- white blouse. She sat on a stool at the bar and ordered a club soda.

Five minutes went by and she walked over to Logan's table. "I know you," she said. "You're Upshur Logan aren't you?"

Logan didn't look up from his computer and said, "I don't give autographs."

"Upshur, I went to Ohio State with you. "I'm Carla Hardy. Don't you remember me?"

Logan looked up "I don't recall you. Someone as beautiful as you I believe I would remember."

Carla blushed, "I was in a history class with you. I kept my head in the books all the time and you never noticed me."

Logan looked again. "Sorry I didn't." Logan paused as her stunning beauty caught his eyes. "Where are my manners? Would you like to join me for dinner, and I will see if I can remember you. You look familiar but I just can't remember you."

They sat had dinner and talked for an hour. Logan told Carla about his career, his ex wife and his kids. Carla told Logan that she had been a teacher in Chicago for awhile but had to leave because she needed a change in her life. She said she would be in town on business for a few days and a girlfriend suggested this restaurant.

The dinner was over Carla got up to leave she asked "Upshur for a business card and whether they could share dinner tomorrow night, if she wasn't being to forward." Logan smiled, pulled out a business card, wrote the hotel phone number and his room and cell numbers on the back and gave her the card. Carla wrote her cell number on a napkin. Carla left the bar before Logan and he didn't see which way she departed the hotel.

Logan left the bar soon after Carla and went to his room. *Carla looks so familiar but I just don't recall her.* It was almost 11:00PM Logan decided to take a shower and get some sleep. Just as he was ready to go in the bathroom, he heard a knock at the door.

"Who is it?" He inquired.

"It's Carla."

Logan opened the door with the chain and saw the beauty with whom he'd had dinner standing in the hall. She must have preformed a quick change. Carla had on black leather pants with a matching vest held fastened by one button and no blouse under it, black gloves, high-heeled boots, black ball cap, and sunglasses and was carrying a gym bag. Her belly button was showing and it was pierced with a small diamond-studded ring. Logan got an instant hard-on when he saw it.

"I did not want to wait until tomorrow to see you again." Carla cooed. "Well, are you going to invite me in or leave me in the hall?"

"Come in please, gulped Logan."

Carla looked in Logan's eyes and said "Now I am being forward. I fantasized about you when we were in college and always thought you were too far away for me to reach. I wanted you badly and then by chance we run into each other, and it brought back feelings. The best thing about a fantasy is the possibility that it may come true."

She grabbed him and pressed her mouth hard into his mouth, probing her tongue deep inside his throat. She could feel the swell mounting in his robe. Carla told Logan it had been a long time since she had been with anyone, but she needed the warmth."

He acknowledged her by saying, "he hadn't been with a woman since his wife."

Carla told Logan to take a shower. She would fix drinks and be ready for him.

When Logan came out of the bathroom Carla had two drinks ready and was stripped to a nice, hot pink lace, Victoria Secret's bra and panty set, and pink elbow-length gloves.

Logan looked at her firm body with her large breasts needing to bust free of the bra.

Logan asked; "Why the gloves?"

Carla explained "I worked in a tannery when I was a teen. The chemicals made my hands sensitive to the touch. The gloves help somewhat but not much."

They drank a little first and then he wrapped his arms around her and kneaded her firm, round, apple-shaped ass, as they explored each other's mouth. He took off her bra to reveal her fat tits poking out at him, and he sucked and gently squeezed them until they were as hard as his dick. She started to caresses his throbbing dick with her hand. He felt as if he could explode at that point. Logan stripped off his robe and Carla took off her panties. Logan looked at her shaved pussy in wonderment.

Carla said "If a bald pussy upsets you, I can leave."

Logan said "No I have never had a shaved one."

They had another drink. Carla asked, "Are you ready for some of this?"

Carla pushed him onto the bed. She mounted his face as to position her pussy over his mouth. Logan kissed on her clit, and ran his tongue around her pussy lips. He felt her body tremble as she grounded her love box into his mouth and had an explosive orgasm.

Carla rolled off, and Logan rolled on top of her his cock trying to find her hole like a snake searching for its niche. She pushed him off. He looked stunned.

She said "Not yet. It is my turn. I will fix you another drink while I'm catching my breath."

She returned to the bed and gave him his drink. She kissed him and pushed him down on the bed. She slowly kissed her way down his body while she was pulling on his dick. She stopped at his peter. She started by pulling the foreskin down and doing an ice cream cone lick around the head. Logan's penis was twitching so much that he thought he was going to come right then. She ran her tongue up and down the shaft of his dick and then took the head into her mouth. She enveloped his penis until it was deep inside her throat. She felt the throb as his cock was ready to erupt, and she stopped. He looked disappointed, until she told him "I want it inside me."

He took another drink and she went to the bathroom to brush her teeth. When she came out of the bathroom, Logan said he felt tired. Carla jumped on his dick and started riding it like a bull in a rodeo. The grief this man had given Carla when she was younger came rushing back as his penis penetrated her vagina. Carla pulled the syringe from between the mattresses where she had hidden it while Logan was in the shower. When he was ready to ejaculate, Logan felt the sharp prick of a needle in his buttocks cheek, his dick went flaccid and his lights went out.

Carla jumped off as Logan's dick went limp inside her. She rifled through Logan's luggage and pulled out four ties. She found in his briefcase the death benefit check in the amount of four million dollars payable to Morgan Renee Roane after the death of her mother Brooke Roane. Logan had two thousand cash in his wallet. She put his laptop and papers into the her gym bag. She stayed in the hot shower for at least a half hour to wash his funk off, and then got dressed in a jogging suit. Carla figured that she'd drugged Logan enough that he would be out for at least a couple hours. Logan awoke at 2:30AM and couldn't move. He tried to scream for help, but nothing came out. He could hear himself in his mind. He could see that his arms were tied to the bed with his neckties, and he was totally immobilized. His body would not respond to his brain's commands. He was spread-eagle and naked, and could not do anything about it.

Carla came into view. "I gave you some special potion to relax you." She asked, "Do you remember me now?"

He tried to yell, "What are you doing bitch?" However, the room remained silent.

"Logan, you brought this upon yourself. Let me explain what I am going to do to you. I have this ziplock bag attached to your balls. A rubber band is attached to your sack, so you don't bleed out right away." She reached into her bag and held up a set of bolt cutters.

Logan screamed and tried to squirm, but he could not move or make a sound.

"Logan, look at me! Do you remember me yet, you bastard." She placed the bolt cutters on his sack. "Remember me motherfucker."

Logan's eyes grew very large and appeared to be popping out of his head.

She snapped his sack off with one quick movement closing the cutters. Logan was in intense pain, but the yelling was only in his mind because no one else could hear him.

It was 4:00AM Carla needed to finish the cleanup. She pulled out the mini vacuum from her gym bag for the floor. She wiped down the place, cleaned the glasses and dumped bleach in the sink and bathtub.

Logan was still lying there, slowly bleeding, and he still couldn't move. She took some tissue dipped it in his blood and left a message on the mirror. The message included the numbers *10/13* and a symbol.

Carla removed the rubber band and let him bleed out. Right before Logan died he remembered a faraway place and something that should not have happened.

Carla thought, "Am *I forgetting something? The air conditioning is set to cold, the do not disturb sign is on the door; I need to call the operator.*"

She picked up the phone dialed *zero.*

"Hotel operator, may I help you."

"This is Ms. Logan in room 623, Cancel the wake up call, and we don't need maid service today."

"Yes, I understand there is an extra charge we will pay it. My husband and I had a long night and need our rest."

Carla hung up. *I want his bowl ring just for a souvenir.*

She opened the door, and turned to the dead body, and said "rest in peace you cock sucking bastard."

CHAPTER 2:
THE FILES

Carla went down the back steps avoiding the elevator. She put her gear into the trunk of her rental car, a blue Chevrolet Malibu. Luckily the car had Washington, DC, tags and she would be able to blend into the surroundings. She started the car and tuned the radio to an oldies' station in DC area. She first needed to find a secluded place along the Potomac River. She stopped along the George Washington Parkway at Alexandria, Virginia near the bike path. She did a quick change into running shoes and ran back the path a short way and threw the opened plastic bag with Logan's scrotum, and testes in the water. *The fish need to eat too*, she thought.

A US Park Police car was pulling up behind her rental when she returned to the car. The officer got out and said, "Ma'am the park is closed at dusk and it isn't a good idea to be out jogging alone at night."

"I apologize, officer I needed to relieve some stress with exercise." She said as she smiled at him.

"Have a nice day ma'am." He stepped back in his cruiser, waited for her to leave the area, and then drove off.

Carla drove onto the Wilson Bridge and over I-295 towards town. She rented a basement apartment from an older lady, in

Northwest DC and could park in the driveway or alley. The lady had said that the area was reasonably safe for that part of town. The lady had also said she needed cash to supplement her social security. She could not accept checks. When Carla arrived at the basement apartment, she took the treasures she'd collected and went inside. Carla opened her briefcase on the kitchen table and searched through the files, until she came upon the one labeled "Upshur Logan." She opened the file, and Logan's whole story was there, from his scholarships to his rise to fame and the injury that that had ended his career. She looked at a newspaper clipping with a picture of him. He'd won an award from the insurance institute about six months ago. She wrote on the file, "expired" and placed it in the done files in the upper part of her briefcase.

Carla looked through her ID collection until she found the passport and Virginia operator's license with her picture and the identity of Morgan Renee Roane. She placed Carla Hardy's identification in Logan's dead file. She opened her diary and wrote down the events of the night. Carla placed the diary and Logan's ring in a fireproof bag that held the trinkets she had collected over the years.

She looked through active files. There were only three left. The next file she came to was labeled with the name of Doddridge Monroe Barbour. Mr. Barbour is a wealthy vice president of the Greenbrier Bank located in Richmond Virginia. The bank is a private financial institution where a million dollar deposit is required to open an account, and a five hundred thousand-dollar minimum was required to keep it open. Morgan Roane's father, Putnam Spencer Roane, had an account at the bank. Carla Hardy had learned of the bank when she'd become friends with Morgan years ago.

Carla looked through the files and found Barbour's private phone number at the bank. She'd paid one thousand-dollars for the unlisted number that only bank clients had. She might as well call and leave a message that she'd be in Richmond tomorrow and would like to see him. She would toss the cell phone on her way to Richmond. Carla figured she had at least twenty-four to thirty hours, before Logan's body would be found. The air- conditioning would make it a little more difficult to set time of death because the rigor mortis and decomposition of the body would be slowed down. Carla thought that after ten of these unfortuninate deaths which the fuck heads all deserved, she was pretty good at clean up.

She looked at the other two files. Both of these guys were in DC area; maybe she could end this adventure this week and put it all to rest for once and for all. Carla secured her files and drifted off into sleep world.

CHAPTER 3:
THE DETECTIVES

Detective Lieutenant Joseph Garbesi of the Arlington County Homicide Unit was sitting in Mary's Diner at 7:00AM Tuesday morning, the same place he set every morning before work for the last twenty-eight years.

Doenay his waitress walked over. "Start with coffee Lieutenant?"

"Yes, please with a number 2." Garbesi asked, "How is your mother?"

Doenay replied, "She is fine are you still soft on her. Why don't you ask her out? I've seen how you look at each other."

Garbesi smiled as Doenay went to get the coffee pot.

Doenay came back to the table with the pot and said, "I have a message for you. Nicholas the cook just gave it to me. Sgt. Tyler has called here for you." She said "you need to turn your cell phone on and call her back as soon as possible."

Sgt. Olivia Tyler was Garbesi's right hand person. She kept him informed and updated. The unit ran smoothly because of her. Garbesi was grooming her to take his place, when he moved to the next rank or to retirement. Olivia Tyler, an attractive woman of five foot eight with brown hair, and brown eyes and has no family. She had never been married and her career was her life. She had out performed all her male counter parts and had moved up quickly. She had earned the respect of the whole force. She'd graduated at the top of her class from Virginia College and had not looked back.

Garbesi reached down and turned on his cell. The tone chimed out that he had a message with a 9-1-1 emergency code. Garbesi dialed his phone and the answer

"Tyler homicide," he heard.

"Liv this is Joe. Have you been trying to reach me? I received a 9-1-1 page."

"Joe, you need to go over to the Goldberg Hotel. Some insurance salesman got himself castrated. The deputy chief wants to know what is going on over at the hotel. I told him you were on the way. It's pretty gruesome according to Detectives Wood and Jefferson."

Sgt. Tyler continued, "The CAT (crime analyze team) is on scene, and the medical examiner's office has been notified." Garbesi wanted to get to the scene before the Crime Analyze Team was gone. He left ten dollars on the table and told Doenay to give Mary, her mother, his best.

Doenay smiled and says "see you tomorrow."

Garbesi arrived at the hotel, flashed his badge and was led to room 623. He met with Kale Wood, the senior detective on the scene. Kale is six foot with blond hair blue eyes and a toned but not overly muscular build. He had been with the force ten years and was sent to the homicide unit four years ago. Wood was sharp as a tack and had a Sherlock Holmes sense about him. Garbesi acknowledged Ted Jefferson. Jefferson had only been with the unit three months. Jefferson looked like he was about to throw his guts up, and Garbesi told him. "Don't puke in my crime scene." Wood motioned with his head to tell Ted it was okay to leave. Wood looked at Garbesi and said, "Jefferson probably doesn't have anything left in his stomach he tossed his cookies twice already." Garbesi asked, "What do we have? And where are we now? Chief Summers wants a briefing as soon as I return to the office."

Wood summarized the incident for Garbesi. "The room is registered to Upshur Logan, an insurance, vice-president from Columbus, Ohio. He was here on a business trip. Security found him this morning, after his company the Hampshire Insurance, also from Ohio, called to inquire about his welfare. He did not call to check in with them, however he made his appointment, it appears, with a Ms. Morgan Roane yesterday to deliver a death benefit check. The check has been cashed and it was for four million dollars. The company requires that the agent call in after a check that large has been issued to the benefactor. Arlington PD was notified, and Corporal J. Braxton and his probationary officer, M. Wirt, were first on the scene. They secured the room and notified us. We haven't touched the body. We are waiting for someone from the ME's office."

Jefferson returned and says, "I apologize, Lieutenant."

Garbesi put his arm around Jefferson's shoulders and said "Don't worry son, It has happened to the best of us. Just make sure you don't mess up the crime scene."

Wood continued, "We have a Winchester address on Ms. Roane. Sgt. Tyler is contacting Winchester PD to see if they can have her contact us. CAT says that the room has been wiped clean, the trash has been emptied, and chemicals or something else has been dumped in the drains. The drinking glasses and other evidence have been collected and taken to the lab. Writing in human blood was found on the mirror. CAT is taking the whole mirror.

The air-conditioning unit was turned to the max. The ME may have a hard time determining time of death."

"Joe, Are you ready to see the body?" asked Randolph Raleigh. Randolph Raleigh was from the ME office and he was checking the body.

Garbesi and Kale nodded at Raleigh and asked him: "What do you know so far?"

Well guys I know that the DB appears to have bled out from the removal of his scrotum. His testes are also missing. The room is so cold that I can't set a TOD. We should know more when La Net looks at him in the office."

La Net Cleopatra Fayette was the head of the ME office.

Raleigh turned to his staff and nodded for them to bag the body and get it to the wagon for transport.

CAT Lieutenant Jones came over asked Garbesi, "Can I take the bed now?"

Garbesi looked at Raleigh. Raleigh said "I'm clear. Do what you need to do."

Wood answered his cell. "Joe the victim had dinner at the bar downstairs Sunday night. The bartender Dennis Mineral remembers him and the lady he was having dinner with. He is coming in early to talk with us."

Garbesi looked at Jefferson and told him to check if there was any video in the hotel. Garbesi finished the sentence with "this hotel is not five stars, he finished but it's not a bed bug inn either: Maybe we can catch a break."

Garbesi' cell phone rang while he was driving to the station.

"Hello, Joe it's Liv Chief Summers Wants to see you when you get to the station. Jefferson tracked down some video from the hotel and is bringing it back to the precinct to review. Wood has met with the bartender and is interviewing him now."

Garbesi said "Liv it sounds like you have it all in order. Do you want to see the chief for me?"

"Not on your life" She replied as she chuckled and hung up the phone.

CHAPTER 4:
THE BANKER

Carla left her apartment house Monday morning at 8:00AM; she figured that she would be in the bank at Richmond by 10 or 10:30. Carla pondered whether she would ever get any sleep when this all was over for good. She tuned the car radio to WTOP the news station as she drove south on I-95. She listened for almost an hour and didn't hear anything about Logan being found. She figured she would not have much time before the hotel maid found his body. She needed to work fast but be accurate.

Carla was dressed conservatively. After all she was Morgan Roane today, and her mother Brooke had passed not long ago. Carla wanted it to appear as if she was still mourning her loss. She'd changed the color of her hair with a red wig, donned a black, designer, above-the-knee dress, with black gloves, shear pantyhose, shaded glasses, and a hat that matched her outfit. She had a black matching clutch bag, which contained the benefit check.

Carla stopped at a WAWA, got a coffee, and dumped the cell she'd given Logan the number for, and called the bank with into the trash.

She arrived on Broad Street in Richmond at approximately 10:18AM and located the Greenbrier Bank tucked away in an obscure location off the main drag. *This bank must be so exclusive,* she thought. No one would ever know it was there, no one who wasn't looking and had the address for it.

She walked into the bank, and the first person to greet her was the receptionist, Ms. June Pleasants, which was anything but pleasant. With a look of disillusion on her face, Ms. Pleasants asked, "May I help you?"

Carla said, "I am Morgan Roane and I want to see Mr. Barbour."

"Do you have an appointment?" The old lady queried.

Carla answered "No; However, I called and left him a message that I would be in town today."

"Are you one of his girlfriends, miss; what's your name was again?" Ms. Pleasants mumbled. "I told him not to bring his floozies in here."

"I am not one of his girls. I'm far from a floozy. My name is Morgan Roane and I am here on business. You can call me Miss Roane! Now may I see Mr. Barbour?"

Ms. Pleasants pointed to a seat. "I'll tell him you are here."

Carla noticed the camera in the lobby pointed at her. She played to the camera by bending over at her seat so the pervert on the monitor could get a cleavage shot and then crossed and re-crossed her legs. The camera was probably trying to look up her dress.

Wayne Cabell, an analyst, at the bank was watching the lobby area and turned on the intercom as soon as Carla walked into the bank. Wayne and Barbour had been drinking buddies for years. Wayne popped his head into Doddridge's office. "Hey, Dodd there is a hot piece of ass in the lobby. I was ready to blow a load under my desk when I saw her. Your aunt is giving her grief. She keeps giving me beaver shots on the camera. She is smoking hot."

Wayne the last time you said "it was a hot bitch she tipped the scales at 325 pounds and was trying out for some wrestling promotion in the south."

"I know Dodd, but she still could suck the skin off your cock."

"You're right, Wayne I never had someone give me skull like that before. Thank goodness I only had to look at the top of her head before I whitewashed her tonsils."

"At least you didn't have to fuck her; she jumped on top of me and dislocated my pelvis. Broke the hotel's bed and I was sore for two weeks. Plus, when she laid on me, I had to move her tits so I could breathe and see the light in the room."

"You loved it Wayne."

"Yeah it was good pussy but I couldn't do a round two."

Dodd looked at Wayne; "I think you would fuck a 2 by 4 if it had a hole in it."

"Wayne replied, "No I would rather have carpet then a hard would floor."

Dodd turned on the lobby camera. Dodd looked at Carla in the camera and felt a chub coming on "What is her name."

I think she said "Roane was her last name."

"I had a message on my phone from her this morning" Dodd said. Wayne do we have a file on her?"

"I already pulled it dude and sent it to your computer."

Wayne briefed Dodd. "She is the daughter of Spencer and Brooke Roane. Spencer owned coal mines in southern West Virginia and Virginia. He was a member of the bank in the Kanawha Valley Branch West Virginia. Spencer died in 1997; his wife Brooke sold the business a year later. Brooke died earlier this year. The Roanes had two children Morgan and her brother Jackson. Jackson died in 2001. Morgan was put on her mother's bank accounts two years ago. Morgan was sent to Europe for school at the age of fifteen. We don't have any more information on her after she went to school. She is worth at least 110 million dollars."

Wayne looked at Dodd and grinned. "I know that look in your eyes. Are we going to attempt a double team on her tonight?"

"No, Wayne you can have whatever I leave."

Wayne looked disappointed. "Let's make a bet Dodd. You make a two hundred thousand dollar a year, salary. Morgan Roane is worth more than you can make in thirty life times. I bet you can't get to first base."

Dodd said "Wayne; I bet you one hundred dollars. I take her to lunch or dinner today. I want to make this interesting. I will bet you five hundred that I bang her tonight."

"Wayne asked, "How in hell are you going to prove that you did her."

Dodd said "I'll take a video camera with me."

"She isn't going to let you video tape having sex with her."

"Wayne, I have this mini camcorder let me worry about it, do we have a bet."

"If you don't take her to dinner or lunch you owe me six hundred dollars".

Dodd and Wayne shook on the bet and Wayne returns to his desk.

Dodd walked to the reception area and told Ms. Pleasants. "Ms Morgan Roane left a message on my private line this morning. Notify me when she gets here."

Ms. Pleasants looked at Dodd and spoke in a low voice. "I know that pervert Wayne was checking her out on the camera and trying to look up her dress."

"Aunt June is that Ms. Roane?"

"Yes, Dodd I was about to call you."

Barbour extends an open hand towards the woman in greeting. "Ms. Roane I am Doddridge Barbour. May I help you?"

"Call me Morgan please. My mother died almost a year ago and I am trying to close out her will. I have an insurance check, which I need to deposit, and I need to find out about any other business. Mom had with your bank.

Dodd led Morgan to his office and offered her a seat. Morgan sat and seductively crossed her legs so as to tease Dodd's wandering eyes. Morgan opened the purse and presented the check for four million dollars to Dodd.

He turned it over and told her she needed to sign and have at least two forms of government identification. While Morgan was signing the check, Dodd hit the intercom button, and Wayne appeared in the office door. "Ms. Roane this is Wayne Cabell one of the banks top analysts. Wayne needs the check and your IDs to verify your account status and the check."

Wayne took the passport, driver's license and check and left the office.

"It shouldn't take any longer than ten minutes to verify; Would you like to stay in my office?"

Morgan set back down.

"I had the staff send me your file after I received your message. We haven't heard very much from you in twenty years. I see your mother added you to her account two years ago."

"When my mother got sick, she had me handle her expenses. She felt that since my brother passed in 2001 and I am the last of the Roane line, something needed to be done with the finances."

They sat in the office for about fifteen minutes making small talk Morgan manipulating her legs as to give glimpses of her sexuality to Barbour. Morgan said "I hope this isn't going to take very much longer. I didn't have breakfast and I am getting hungry."

Dodd looked at this as an opening. "Could I make up for the inconvenience we've caused by taking you to lunch?"

Morgan gave Dodd a girlish blush. "Mr. Barbour, I will take you up on that offer."

"Wayne knocked and apologized for taking a long time. The branch in West Virginia had a difficult time in locating the signature cards. They are faxing the cards to me. Here are all your account numbers; we have to put a hold on the insurance payment; however, you still have access to your accounts. We should know by this afternoon."

Wayne left the room.

"Mr. Barbour it's 11:50 now, How about a late lunch about 2:00PM?" Morgan said; "I can freshen up and take a nap."

"Morgan gave him the cell number from a new throwaway phone, which she'd purchased this morning from a 7-11. Dodd handed Morgan his business card.

Wayne came into Dodd's office after Morgan left and gave him five twenty dollar bills. "I have to hand it to you, Dodd; you have always been the smoothest talker I've known.

"She made it easy, Wayne. She practically gave it up in here. She kept showing me her legs and giving me brief glances of breast."

"Dodd remember to take the camcorder. I want my five hundred dollars worth."

Dodd notified Ms. Pleasants that he would be out the rest of the afternoon.

"Be careful Doddy, You are all I have left of my sister."

"I will Aunt June," Dodd replied, as he pecked her on the cheek.

Dodd called the phone number Morgan had given him. "Ms. Roane, this is Dodd Barbour I'm leaving the bank now. "Would you like to meet me at Tomas' Café in Shockoe Bottom?"

"Dodd I had fallen asleep could you pick me up in about twenty minutes? I am at the Chisel Wick hotel on Midlothian."

"I will be there shortly." Dodd replied.

Dodd and Wayne had taken women to the Chisel Wick. He wondered why a rich woman would want to stay in a dive like that. She just wasn't familiar with the Richmond area, Dodd believed.

Dodd pulled into the hotel lot at 2:30PM and called Morgan.

"Dodd I'm still not ready. It will be another ten minutes can you come to room 326? I don't have anything stronger than soda. You can have a drink while you wait."

"I will be up in a few minutes," Dodd hung up and called Wayne to tell him that he'd been invited up to Morgan's hotel room. "Wayne, have my money tomorrow" Dodd laughed and hung up.

Morgan pulled a soda from the refrigerator and got a cup of ice. She popped the top on the soda and put some powder in the can and some in the glass. She poured the pop, and then a knock came at the door. She stirred the soda so the powder would not be detected. Morgan opened the door, invited Dodd to sit, and gave him the drink.

Dodd couldn't take his eyes off her. She was wearing a silk-type knee-length robe that was only fastened with a tie around her waist and matching gloves. The robe was see-through He noticed her perky nipples on her large boobs trying to jump out at him and the hidden treasure, black, bikini panties she was wearing. He felt a throbbing jump in his pants.

Morgan played his stares off and said, "You noticed my gloves. The doctor told me to always wear gloves because of chemical burns on my hands. The gloves help the healing."

Dodd watched Morgan's round, apple-shaped ass as she turned to chain the door.

He gulped his drink and refilled the glass. He made a poor attempt of not letting her notice him staring as his aching cock tried to break free of its confines.

Morgan came over to the chair and straddled him. She pressed her mouth hard to his and her tits to his chest. "Dodd you are probably not used to a female being aggressive but I like men and I feel that bulge in your crotch. Do you want to fuck me before we eat or after or before and after?"

Dodd blushed, and for the first time in his life, he was speechless.

"We can just go eat if you aren't interested" she said and she got off him. "I saw the rise in your pants when I went to your office. I thought you were aroused. I didn't mean to offend you."

"Morgan the question caught me off guard."

Morgan turned and went toward the bathroom. Dodd, "you have a few minutes to make your decision."

Dodd took of his suit jacket and put the video camera under it, pointing it at the bed. *I must be the luckiest man in the world;* he thought. *I am going to have sex with a beautiful woman and an extra five hundred bucks in my pocket tomorrow.*

When Morgan came from the bathroom, the robe was gone and she was standing in front of Dodd in her panties and gloves. She went to him and started kissing him. She kissed down his chest, removing his shirt and unlacing his belt. She dropped his pants to his ankles and pulled down his boxers. She squatted in front of him like a catcher would at home plate. She started working his manhood with her hands and teasing with her tongue until he became fully erect, which she noted did not take but a few seconds. She thought to herself *he is a good nine to nine and a half inches and thick. It's a shame he has to die.*

Morgan started to go up and down the side of his shaft with her lips as if she was jacking him off with her mouth. She looked up at him. He looked as if he was going into a trance. "Dodd have you ever had a grease job?"

"No I am not sure."

"You might want to lie on the bed this is going to make you weak in the knees."

Dodd thought *we will be in front of the camera.*

Morgan continued to work his shaft and play with his balls. She moved to the head and popped it in and out of her mouth quickly. She moved her mouth down his penis and created suction in her mouth that drove Dodd to the brink of ecstasy when she started to withdraw. She repeated this action fast and slow. She put so much saliva on his dick that it shined in the light. She stopped when Dodd felt the back of her throat. She rubbed his cock head on the soft pallet of the roof of her mouth and paused a minute, and he heard her pass the gag reflex. She moved her mouth down slowly like a snake taking in its prey. He looked down and her mouth was all the way down to his pubic bone. She massaged the skin between his sack and asshole. Dodd groaned with pleasure. She knew at this point she could do what she wanted with him. However she wanted to enjoy torturing him with pleasure. Just as he was ready to explode in her mouth, she pulled off and collared his cock with her hand. "I don't want you to come yet."

She stood up and pulled off her panties. "It's my turn."

He saw her bare pussy and smiled, thinking of Wayne's analogy of hardwood versus carpeted floors. Dodd thought, *what the hell? Any woman who can give head like Morgan does can have anything she wants.*

She straddled his face and began grinding her pussy into his mouth. He started to nibble at the clit and then flick it with his tongue. He totally got into it. When she started shuttering and was ready to orgasm, Dodd stuck a finger in her butthole and his tongue in her love canal. She ground her pelvis so hard into his face that he thought *she would break his nose.* She came with such convulsions that her love juices were secreted on his face. She fell off of him and was in a total state relaxation.

She was lying on the bed and he rolled over on top of her, she was brought back to reality. "Not yet big boy. Go wash your face. I will pour us a soda. Then I am going to ride you like you never have been ridden."

Dodd came back from the bathroom, and she pushed him down on the bed. She slowly lowered herself down onto his hips until his cock disappeared inside her. She could feel it up in her stomach and thought *this will be over soon. I'll deal with the discomfort.*

She brought him to the boiling point when she got off and told him to doggy style. She got on all fours and stuck her rump in the air. Dodd entered her from the back and got excited about her firm ass slapping into his abs. He attempted to move his dick up to her asshole. She stopped bucking back on him and said, "Not now after we eat. I want you to come in me." She rolled over on her back and prepared to take his throbbing penis.

Dodd felt that he could not hold off anymore. Once he entered Morgan's vagina he pumped twice and then felt a stick in his neck and the liquid from the syringe flow into his body. Morgan pushed him off her and went to the bathroom. She brushed her teeth until the enamel was almost gone and gargled for at least ten minutes.

She came back into the bedroom, opened the closet door and pulled out strips of bed sheet that she'd sliced up earlier. She tied Dodd to the bed, just in case he woke up before her shower was done. She stayed in the steamy shower for about an hour.

Morgan performed her extensive clean up ritual, put her clothes on and sat in a chair by the bed writing in her diary.

Dodd is a great lover. I have never come with anyone like I did with him. It's too bad

he set his own fate years ago. I almost regret what I have to do, however; he brought

it upon himself to pay for his past and any future transgressions.

Morgan looked over and saw Dodd's eyes flickering and closed her diary.

Dodd could not move no matter how hard he tried.

"Dodd don't bother. You can not move. The drugs I gave you will hold you in check for a long time. If you look down at your genitals, you'll notice that there is a wire wrapped around your penis and one around your sack. Do you know what they are?"

"Oh, I forgot you can't answer." Morgan explained "It's a garrote, a very effective assassins' weapon. It is clean and quite. I have put a rubber band on the bases of your penis and bag. I have plastic lunch bags to protect your jewels, and I feed them to the animals. You wouldn't bleed out, at least not right away. All I have to do is pull these handles." She tightened the garrote and then released it.

Dodd could fell the wire cutting into his flesh. *He wondered why the hell she was doing this to him.*

"Dodd I found your video camera. What were you going to do? Sell it on the Internet, or maybe take it back to show Wayne?

I know that pervert was looking up my dress. I kind of wished you would have brought him with you. I might have made him fuck you in the ass."

"I reviewed the tape. We could have made two hot porn stars. No one will ever see it. Your womanizing days are over. Do you remember me, asshole breath?" Morgan came close to Dodd's ear and whispered in it.

He remembered and then had a look of shock before she snapped the garrote first around his penis and then his sack.

"I told you it would be quick and silent. You'll bleed slowly at first, when the bands become slippery with blood. They will pop off, and the blood will flow freely. They should find you in the morning. You might die of shock before; in any case, you can't do a thing about it. I have adjusted the air. I hope you don't get to cold. I am taking your watch to remember you. I hope you don't mind, prick." Morgan dipped a tissue in his blood and scrolled *11/13* and a symbol on the hotel mirror.

Morgan decided to go up Chamberlain Avenue to route 301 to Maryland. She would dump the contents of the bags and the cell phone in the Potomack River before she crossed the Nice Bridge into Maryland.

CHAPTER 5:
THE PRIEST

Garbesi arrived back at the precinct around 11:30AM. Sgt. Tyler met him as soon as he got off the elevator. They talked as they walked towards the lieutenant's office.

"Joe I hate to hit you with this all at once. Chief Summers wants you to brief him by 12:45PM about were the investigation on Logan's death is going. He is going to have a news conference at 1:30PM."

"Liv, the body was just found this morning and the ME took him to the morgue about an hour ago."

"Joe, Mr. Logan was a celebrity of sorts. He played pro football for several years. The chief made this a high profile case and has asked the ME to put a rush on the autopsy. You and I look at a homicide as a homicide. You know how the political system works with the brass."

"Father Berkeley McDowell wants to talk to you she added. He says he won't talk to anyone else."

Garbesi looked at Tyler, "Did he give you a hint of what he needs to talk about?"

"He said he wants to report a rape said Tyler."

"The rape unit is down the hall."

"I told him that, Joe. He said it involves Logan and it happened about twenty years ago."

"I still don't understand why he wants to talk to me. The statute of limitations has run out long ago. Logan is dead now, so it won't matter anyway."

"Joe maybe you should listen to what he has to say. Show him in and send in Detective George Calhoun to take notes."

"Father McDowell, have a seat. I am Lt. Joe Garbesi. I don't completely understand how you know about Logan's death. His body was just found this morning, and the press won't be notified of his identity until the family is notified."

McDowell spoke softly; "Logan and I are from the same hometown of Valley Cove, West Virginia near the Virginia border in the south. Logan called me on Sunday when he arrived in town. He wanted to talk about an incident that happened about twenty years ago. I was supposed to meet with him at 9:00AM to discuss it. Hotel personnel told me he had been murdered and that you were in charge. I think what I need to tell you may be pertinent to his murder. Logan and I, along with eleven other boys were involved in a rape about twenty or so years ago. I have asked for forgiveness and am still asking for forgiveness today."

"A girl lived in our town named Darla Knapper. She was a very beautiful fifteen years old. I believe she was mixed with Mingo Indian, black, white, and Italian heritage. She had caramel-colored, smooth skin, and her body was well developed for her age. It was rumored that she was easy, sexually. Her stepbrother named Clay Mercer, came to school in April or May 1987 and sold lottery tickets for fifty bucks to have sex with Darla. He said Darla knew about it and was going to get 50 percent of the money for it. Everyone who put in money would get some action; there were thirteen boys who put in money. We ranged in ages from fourteen to nineteen years old. The lots were drawn, and each of us received a number. Darla was taken to an end-of-school party by the senior jock, Mason Hancock. He also had lottery ticket #1. He took Darla to the beach by the lake about an hour into the party. When Darla had his penis in her mouth, the other twelve of us, plus her stepbrother came out of the woods and started clapping at their performance. Darla had a look of shock on her face. Mason told her, "If you bite me bitch. You'll regret it."

He pulled his member from her mouth and pushed her down on the sand and had intercourse until he finished. When she tried to fight he slapped her in the face. It became apparent that she was not a willing participant.

"Number two in the lottery was Mason's younger brother Grant. I believe he was fourteen at the time. He took her in much the same way but he wasn't brutal with Darla. The third guy had his way with her and she continued to fight. Her stepbrother whispered something in her ear and it looked as if the fight in her was gone. The fourth guy took her anally. I got sick and left, and went to the woods and puked my gut out my lottery number was twelve. Ritchie Taylor who was number thirteen must have had an attack of conscience and followed me. I went back in the early hours the next morning. I could see Darla was still alive. She was naked lying on the sand and appeared cold from the mourning dew. I covered her with a jacket and dress. I found on the beach. Darla tried to report the incident a week after it happened. The sheriff was Lincoln Hancock, the grandfather of Mason and Grant. A phony investigation was conducted and everyone at the party was questioned but no one saw anything."

"Father, this is some story but what does it have to do with Mr. Logan's death?"

"Logan wanted to talk with me because nine of the thirteen guys that were involved in the rape have been murdered or are missing. Plus, Darla's stepbrother went missing three weeks after the rape. I saw Clay a few days after the incident. He had a black eye, and his arm was in a sling. We were told that he ran away because his father beat him. Mason Hancock disappeared two months later. Darla supposedly killed her stepfather a month after that, and she was committed to a sanitarium. I have kept extensive files and tabs on all of those involved since the day it happened. A total of eleven, now twelve people connected to this have disappeared or have been murdered. I called Logan, and found out that he was going to be in town. I did not explain what I wanted to talk about, but he agreed to see me."

Joe put his hand to his mouth as if he were in thought. "Where is this Darla now?"

"She died in a fire in the asylum in West Virginia in early 2002," explained the priest.

Garbesi twitched his fingers tapping them together in front of his mouth; "Do you think someone is exacting revenge for her or do you think she may still be alive?"

"I don't know. I said she died in a fire. Two bodies were found after the fire a male and a female. Two females were unaccounted for and one body was never recovered. All the records were destroyed during the fire, so no dental X-rays were available to compare. Darla and the other female I can't recall the other girl's name were the only two females not accounted for," the priest continued. "The second female was in the asylum because of a fascination with fire. The state wanted to clear the case fast so they blamed the fire on her and declared Darla's body burned beyond recognition and closed the case."

"The second female can we find out her name?" asked the detective.

"It is somewhere in my files, I will look for it," replied the priest. "Darla had family and friends back at the Cove. I am scared," added the father. "I know, I am not a saint. I am trying to make up for past sins. I know that I am now on a very short list."

"Father McDowell, will you excuse use for a minute? Liv, come in here please.

The father had a seat outside the office.

"What do you think, Calhoun?"

"Joe, the story sounds viable."

"Calhoun, write his statement, determine if he is a nut, a suspect, or a lead. Liv, I need you to check with Wood and Jefferson. See if they have developed anything from the video at the hotel or from the bartender. I would like the two of you also to work on any names that McDowell gives in the statement. Liv, I also need you to check with Dr. Fayette at the ME office. Ascertain when we can come to her office."

"Joe the family has been notified" said Liv.

Joe stepped out of the office. "Father McDowell, I need to go to a meeting with the chief. I need you to go with detective Calhoun and write a statement and may we have copies of your files."

"Lt. Garbesi, anything to help you."

"Father, don't leave anything out of your statement."

Calhoun pointed to a chair near his desk. "Please have seat I'll be there shortly."

Garbesi sat in Chief Summers' office for ten minutes waiting. Garbesi thought *some things never change.* He and Summers had gone to the police academy together. Summers loved making people wait. He kissed a lot of political ass to get his position. Garbesi thought about the rumor that Summers had a funeral escort to National Airport. The funeral was for a political figure's wife. He'd started crying and helped carry her coffin to the plane. He would do anything to get his face on TV. He had pictures in his office of himself shaking hands with three different presidents and various foreign dignitaries.

"Joe, sorry to keep you waiting, Do we have anything on the Logan murder that we can give the press?"

"Chief the body was discovered this morning. We can release his name. The family has been told of his death and that it was a murder, but not given any of the particulars."

"Garbesi I am going to introduce you as the lead investigator for the news."

Officer Natalie Wetzel the public relations representative for the department came into the office.

"Joe, Officer Wetzel will brief you on your statement to the press. Tell her what you have. The press conference is in about ten minutes."

CHAPTER 6:
THE PRESS CONFERENCE/
TUESDAY AFTERNOON

Morgan Roane's persona was closed out with the file on Doddridge Barbour. Carla assumed the identity of Marion Greene today, in case someone needed to see identification. She hoped that she could finish her mission before the end of the week. Marion hated staying in the same area for a long period of time. However, it just happened that the last two targets were still in this region.

She was out picking up supplies for her next conquest. She had heard on the radio that a dead body had been found in Arlington, but the identity and other facts were being with held until next of kin had been notified. A press conference was scheduled for around 1:30PM this afternoon.

Marion stopped around 1:00PM in a diner in Arlington to grab a bite and catch the news conference on TV.

The waitress came over to her and asked: "How many?"

Marion said, "Just one, May I set at the bar?"

The waitress smiled gave her a menu and said, "Help yourself."

Marion ordered an iced tea and a caesar salad.

"Ma'am may I ask you a question?" the waitress said. "Are you a model? You are one of the most beautiful women I have ever seen."

Marion smiled and blushed; she had noticed the girl's name tag. "I am not a model Doenay. You have a beautiful and unusual name."

"Thank you, my mom gave it to me. She said my dad liked the name."

Doenay turned to go retrieve the order when the news came on the TV. She stopped to turn the set louder. She stood there to listen to the broadcast.

The reporter appeared on the screen and announced, "The body of a murdered man was found in the Goldberg hotel in Arlington Virginia this morning. Now let's go to Deputy Chief of Police Summers for an update on the breaking news."

The mike crackled as Chief summers spoke, "Today, the body of Upshur Logan was discovered, murdered at the Goldberg Hotel. Mr. Logan had missed several appointments and did not check in with his firm. Calls concerning his welfare were received at the hotel. Staff checked his room and discovered the body. Lt. Joe Garbesi is leading the investigation."

The detective took the stage. "All that we can tell you right now is that Mr. Logan was murdered sometime between Sunday and this morning. The lab is working now to narrow the time and cause of death. We have several people who may have seen him last we are speaking with them. The investigation is continuing."

Doenay turned to Marion, "I am sorry I'll get your order.

She returned "here's your order miss and I apologize again."

"Don't worry honey. Do you know that detective?" asked Marion.

Doenay said, "Joe has been coming in here for breakfast since I was a little girl. He is kind of like a father to me. I never knew my real father and Joe and my mother Mary have always been close. When ever mom needed something Joe was there. He helped her buy this place. He never forgot a birthday, or graduation, and he even gave me away at my wedding. When my husband died, he was there to comfort Mom, me and my son. I think him and Mom are secretly in love but can't stand to be together."

"Doenay, you favor that detective somewhat. Do you think he might be your father? I see how you paid closed attention when he was speaking."

"No, he is just a good friend of the family. I also know that he is a top cop, very good at what he does. He has accommodations and metals for the work he has done for this county, as far as closing cases, and services in the military."

Doenay walked away Marion could see that she'd made the young woman think.

Marion thought that if this detective was as good as the waitress said she might have to move up her agenda. But she couldn't get sloppy.

Marion left $10.00 for a $7.50 tab. "Thank you for your kind remarks, Doenay, and think about what I said. Good luck."

CHAPTER 7:
SQUAD CONFERENCE ROOM

Garbesi spent another fifteen minutes with Chief Summers after the press conference. Then he went to his office. Sgt. Tyler had the dry erase board set up in the conference room and had already started writing on it. Detectives Wood, Jefferson, and Calhoun were already seated in the room.

Sgt. Tyler started the briefing by pointing to the board. "Lieutenant let's bring you up to date on our new information," She said. "I received the prelim report from CAT. The only evidence is the mirror. No finger prints were found in the room, including Logan's prints. Whoever did this appeared to have vacuumed the floor and poured chemicals in the tub and sink. The bathroom floor was even bleached. There were semen stains on the bed sheets, but it was not matched to the victim and the lab felt that they were old because they were degraded from laundering. We can't rule out that there was a second male in the room."

The numbers *10/13* and an unknown symbol were written on the mirror in the victim's blood. DNA matched Logan. We don't know what it means. I contacted the gang unit, and they're checking the numbers and symbol in their database. No one in the gang unit recognized either. We are not sure what the symbol is yet."

"The Winchester PD called me back. They have no record of Ms. Roane or the given address. Wood, you're next."

Wood walked to the front of the room. "I spoke to the bartender, a Dennis Mineral. He remembers a very attractive light skinned lady with dark hair having dinner with Logan on Sunday night. She was dressed like she'd just stepped off a Fredrick's of Hollywood catalog, according to him. The waitress Joan Webster remembers Logan calling his dinner companion, Carla. Webster didn't get a last name. Ms. Webster said Logan came to the restaurant alone and believes that the woman approached him. Logan and the woman talked as if they were old friends. The waitress recalled the pair talking about college and thinks they may have been in school together."

"Logan played college football at Ohio State and pro football for a few years and she may have recognized him as a ball player. He had alcohol with dinner, and she had soda. Logan paid for the meal with a company card. They left separately about ten minutes apart, sometime before 11:00PM."

"The only video in the bar is at the cash register and outside the entrance. Both the bartender and waitress remembered that the woman wore elbow-length gloves that she never took off. I sent the video to the lab from the bar entrance. She was wearing a hat and sunglasses. The bartender and waitress identified the woman on the tape as Logan's dinner companion. Reggie, the video tech, is going to try to work different angles. However he can't make any promises."

Liv looked at Jefferson, "Do you have anything to add?"

Jefferson stood up, "I requested security video from stairwells and hallways from Sunday until this morning. Sunday at around 11:05PM a woman went to Logan's hotel room and left his room at approximately 4:30AM Monday morning. The hotel clerk remembers that she received a call around 4:20AM canceling the wake-up call request. The caller said she was Mrs. Logan. The call was not recorded."

"The woman on the video was dressed all in black, jeans, black vest, baseball cap, and gloves to her elbows. She also wore sunglasses. The bartender and the waitress said she looked similar to the woman Logan had dinner with but wouldn't swear they were the same person. They also questioned how she could have changed so fast because it was only ten minutes or less after Carla left the bar and this woman appeared at Logan's room. I also sent the video to Reggie."

"Everyone registered in the hotel is being asked if they saw anyone or anything, Jefferson concluded."

Sgt. Tyler addressed the room. "I brought Calhoun in here because I believe he is developing a lead." Liv looked at Calhoun. "Do you have something for us?"

"I think the clergy statement has some merit." Calhoun looked at the lieutenant and spoke. "I think we should follow up on his story. I have a list of the thirteen people who were involved in the alleged rape of Darla Knapper. The priest had a file with the names and stories of all of the involved parties. He has followed them through the newspapers and Internet since the day of the heinous act. He is according to him, trying to make up for past sins."

"All of the people on the list were associated with each other. It may be a coincidence. The news clippings in the priest's files reported that ten, now eleven of the people on the list have died under suspicious circumstances, were murdered or went missing. Ten of the men were actually involved in the alleged rape and her stepbrother was the supposed facilitator. Ms. Knapper may have died herself in a fire five years ago."

"The second woman who was involved with Ms. Knapper at the sanitarium was Morgan Roane. Roane's name matches the name of the insurance client that Logan supposedly saw Monday. I would like to have our dispatchers send an administrative message to the involved agencies to obtain any reports on these cases. I would like to follow up on Ms. Knapper. Maybe someone is exacting revenge on her behalf."

Liv said, "Joe I have read Father McDowell's statement, and I think it is worth a closer look."

"I don't want to waste allot of time on a wild goose chase. I'll trust your judgment. I know McDowell is one of the three men left from the rape, try to locate the other two people and speak with them," said Garbesi. Lieutenant,

Calhoun interrupted "excuse me; I thought you may want to know that Doddridge Barbour who lives in Richmond, Virginia is one of them. The third man is named Ritchie Taylor with an address here in Arlington."

"I'm impressed Calhoun with your initiative to follow up." Garbesi appeared to be thinking and said "I went to the FBI academy with a Lt. Glendale McCaffery of the Richmond investigative unit. I'll get his office numbers. Call him. He might be able to help with this Barbour guy. Tell him Barbour's name came up in a murder investigation. We would like to question him. We request Richmond PD be involved in the query." Garbesi went to his office to get the number.

He came back five minutes later, "Calhoun, call him now."

The detective left to make the call.

"Wood, have Mr. Mineral and Ms. Webster sit down with a sketch artist for a composite. Before anything is released to the press, go through proper channels.

Jefferson, continue interviewing hotel guests and staff for further leads. If you need help take Carl Harrison with you, he comes back from vacation tomorrow."

The meeting was about to adjourn when Calhoun came back. "Lt. Garbesi, I called, and McCaffery's phone rolled over to Corporal Carol Ibis's desk. She told me McCaffery was on a call. She would pass on the message. When I mentioned Doddridge Barbour, she paused and said she would have McCaffery call as soon as possible. Ibis called our dispatchers to confirm I was who I claimed to be."

Joe's cell phone chimed.

"Garbesi, this is McCaffery. My office said you have been working on a homicide and needed to speak to me about one of our citizens, a Doddridge Barbour.

"Yes, Glen, his name came up in our investigations. We need to speak to him."

"Joe, you'll need a medium. Mr. Barbour was found murdered in a hotel room in Richmond this morning. I can't discuss particulars on the cell."

"Glen, can I send a detective down tomorrow and see what information we can share?"

"I will clear it with the brass, answered McCaffery. Joe do you have the detective's name?"

"I will send George Calhoun." Garbesi closed his phone. "George, put in a request for an unmarked car in the morning and go to Richmond to see Lt. McCaffery. He will be waiting for you. Mr. Barbour is no longer with the living. He has been murdered,

Calhoun call me or Liv ASAP. Finish a draft of the admin messages before you leave tonight. Liv, check them over and send them with request for priority responses. I will talk to McDowell, and attempt to locate Ritchie Taylor. I'll offer them protective custody."

"Joe," Sgt. Tyler said, "we have to see Dr. Fayette in the ME office at 9:00AM tomorrow. I'll do the follow-up on Calhoun's phone calls and admin messages.

Sgt. Tyler and Garbesi were the only two left in the room. Joe, "Do you think that we may be depending too much on Calhoun? Since he has been in the unit, he coasts by, with doing as little as he can, shoveling his work off on others and just collecting a pay-check. When evals come up at the end of the year, his would not be passing."

"Liv, I set Calhoun down and told him this was his last chance before I recommend he be returned to street duty. I gave him some responsibility; if he fails it's on me."

CHAPTER 8: THE MEDICAL EXAMINER OFFICE

Doctor La Net Cleopatra Fayette waited in her office for Garbesi and Tyler to arrive at 9:00AM Wednesday morning. Dr. Fayette stood five foot two inches and weighed in at two hundred and ten pounds with a round pie-shaped face and the disposition of a teddy bear. She was one of the best liked and most highly respected people in the field of forensics. People who met her for the first time were attracted to her magnetism and ability to make a person feel full of life. She could speak four languages and graduated tops in her class at the Virginia Commonwealth (VCU) and Georgetown Medical Universities. The labs from the FBI, other states, federal agencies, and a cable channel tried to steal Dr. Fayette's expertise because of her relentless pursuit of the truth.

She wasn't always as happy as she had been in the last six months. She'd grown up in small Tazewell Virginia. Her mother had died when she was young and her father had kept the family together. He'd instilled in her and her seven siblings that, no matter how tough life can be, a person with faith and integrity can set his or her own path to create a future of failure or achievement. La Net, being the youngest, was her father's little princess. No one in the family was the favorite. La Net, being the youngest, and smallest, was the most protected by the rest of the family. She'd had a fairly happy childhood with all her siblings and father watching over her. She'd demonstrated her prowess in school by learning to speak two languages in thee years. She'd also become the first black woman to be voted senior class president and homecoming queen in the same year. She'd weighed only 107 pounds back then.

She later recalls how proud her whole family had been of her. She'd come home and told her dad that she was the first Afro-American woman to ever achieve this in her school. La Net, would remember that this was the first and only time her dad had become curt with her. "La Net, you are my princess and I am not upset with you." He told her.

He'd called a family meeting. "I want to explain a philosophy that has been handed down to me through the years. You may keep the philosophy or create your own. Your mother and I have had ancestors in this country for over two hundred years. Every male has fought for this country both on this soil and in foreign theaters; some have spilled blood for freedom. The right to be called American has been earned by all of them. We don't need to be hyphenated. We don't need a label to distinguish us from one American to another. Remember we can be stronger when we stand united and not divided. You will still run into bigots and prejudice because of color, sex, or religion. Just remember who you are and the sacrifices that have been made for you. Don't stereotype people: not everyone is bad. There are still people in the world and this country of all races who will try to drive a wedge and try to divide us as a nation by continuing the hatred between the races. Prejudice is not inherited. It is learned."

She would always remember his speech and tried to adhere to it.

La Net made an error in judgment at least that is how she looked at it in her senior year. She became pregnant. The pregnancy wasn't planned. Her family supported her, and so did the father of her child. She would never look at her son, Brian as an error. The son's father supported them at first and disappeared after the baby was born. He would show up to see the baby once in a while and to get a piece of La Net's pie. He started whoring around until he had four children and four different baby's mommas. La Net was offered scholarships from several different colleges but decided to go to VCU because Richmond, Virginia was closer to Tazewell and family who had been keeping her son.

La Net had several bad relationships with men in which she had been abused both physically and mentally. The men told her she was fat and stupid and that her child was a bastard. She was driven so far into depression that she started to believe them. She started to eat and hit the three hundred and ten pound mark on the scale.

She could put on the façade at work; no one knew there was a problem. Four years ago, the Arlington Police were called by neighbors to a domestic disturbance at her home. Detective Wood, then a senior patrol officer, was one of the cops on the scene. Wood removed her son from the scene. The other police officers dealt with La Net and the asshole man.

La Net could have lost her job over the situation; however Kale Wood and several other officers spoke up for her. Once the man was removed from her house, she decided it was best for her and her son to swear off men. She figured that all men just wanted in her panties or a blow job and could give a shit about her or anyone else. She hadn't seen Wood since that night. He would call her house once in a while and take Brian out to a ball game. Wood asked her first if it was all right to take Brian out. La Net figured that, since she'd moved to Arlington. Wood was the closest thing to a father figure Brian had, and he seemed to be a positive influence, so she always let her son go. She never thought that she and Wood could ever hook up.

A year and a half ago, Wood had shown up in the coroner's office as a detective. It was late and time for La Net to go home. Everyone else had left for the evening. She'd had call a neighbor to make arrangements for her son.

She was already pissed about Wood's timing, but she understood somewhat about police work. You try to make timely appointments but it doesn't always work out. She wanted to talk with him about an outing her son was having at school. He was supposed to bring his father, and since Wood had become a sort of big brother La Net wanted to ask him to take Brian. She had only talked to Wood on the phone since the night of the domestic and had not had a face to face. She was glad to see Wood, and her anger subsided.

Wood was investigating a death of an old man. To close the case, it needed to be determined whether his demise was accidental or homicide. La Net and Wood dressed in aprons, donned masks, and put latex gloves on their hands. La Net at the time had to use the metal crutches with half collars around her arms because of the weight she carried on her small frame. The two of them went to the autopsy room where the body was already out on a steel gurney. La Net explained that she had already had done a preliminary. La Net told Wood that she believed the death to be accidental, and she wanted to show him her reasons.

Wood made a smart ass remark in a Jamaican accent, "yes I see Madam Cleo."

La Net became pissed again for two reasons no one ever used her middle name, and Madam Cleo referred to some quack physic on TV commercials. She gave Wood a death stare and thought *maybe he is an asshole like the rest of the men.* The room was quiet and she continued with her explanation of the death.

Wood made the crack about Madam Cleo again, and La Net turned and cracked him in the shin with her crutch.

Wood fell to the floor in agonizing pain. "Why did you hit me?"

"You're making fun of me," La Net replied.

"I thought doctors are supposed to heal not hurt."

"You pushed it detective," La Net squawked.

La Net helped him to his feet and led him to a couch in her office.

"La Net, I'm sorry you're offended by my dumb comments. I just wanted to get your attention. I talk to you on the phone and know you through your son. I want to know you better as a person. I thought maybe you would ask if you could come out with me and Brian, but you never do. I would like to take you to dinner, La Net."

"Why didn't you just ask instead of acting like an ass?"

"La Net I don't know how to talk to women. Besides I thought, why would someone as smart and as hot as you want to go out with a country bumpkin like me?"

La Net laughed and "I thought what would a six foot white man with beautiful eyes and a great body ever see in a short five foot two inch fat black woman like me."

Wood looked real deep into her eyes and said "I didn't realize you were short."

She leaned down and kissed him on the cheek. He pulled her back and down and kissed her passionately on the mouth.

The relationship began and had endured this helped her confidence and his. Brian had benefitted by having two people who care about his well-being. La Net had lost more than a hundred pounds and no longer used the crutches. She didn't look at men in the same way and understood that they don't all just want pussy or head all the time.

Shed figured this out after her and Kale had been going out for three months and she'd asked him to stay with her one evening. Brian had gone to West Virginia to his grandfather for the weekend.

She'd asked Kale, "When are we going to have sex?"

Kale looked at her in his boyish way and honestly said, "My cinnamon princess, I was waiting for you to tell me when you were ready to move to the next level of our relationship."

La Net smiled and told him, "She loved him." She also told him, "Kale I like oral sex and I am told that you white people invented it."

They both laughed.

Kale was gentle with her and made sure she had an orgasm that night and every time they made love.

Kale was happy. He loved his new family and spoke up more Brian's grades had improved immensely.

The intercom beeped; interrupting Le Net's thoughts. She pushed the button. Ann the receptionist's voice said Dr. Fayette, "Lt. Garbesi and Sgt. Tyler are here to see you."

"Show them in Ann."

Garbesi and Tyler hugged La Net as a greeting.

Dr. Fayette addressed both of them. "Have seat please. I don't know were the chief gets his pull but I was here until 9:00PM finishing with Mr. Logan. Evidently Chief Summers called someone upstairs, and I had to push the other cases to the side to finish this one and send evidence to the lab. The lab is going to rush also and put this case in front instead of the three weeks wait. Results are supposed to be in this morning."

"When Logan's body came in before, we washed him. The nasal cavity, and inside of the mouth were swabbed. He didn't completely bleed out; we collected enough blood for a toxicology screen. We then took pictures to see underlying bruising that isn't visible to the naked eyes. I noticed a gel-type substance under the foreskin of his penis which was also swabbed. The body was washed and caught in a bucket. I located a needle puncture mark in his right buttocks, where there was a small clot to stop the bleeding. Metal fragments were located near the injury site. The contents of his stomach were collected."

La Net asked the two to step over to her lighted X-ray boards. She had already posted the pictures up. "Look at the first picture. You're looking at Logan's chest area." She pointed to the image. "There appear to be handprints on both side of his chest, as if he was being held down. Here are pictures of where the bonds were on him, this picture is his hips, and this is from the skull and facial areas. It doesn't look as if he fought against any of these marks because they are not deep. If he'd fought against his attacker the marks would be more pronounced."

Garbesi asked; "What are the marks alongside his hips and jaws?"

Dr. Fayette said, "If I were a betting woman. I'd say they are thighs. Let's sit; I believed that maybe Mr. Logan had sex before he died."

Tyler asked; "How are you going to prove that; his genitals are gone."

"His penis is still intact, so I decided to fillet it," replied the doctor.

Joe squirmed in his chair.

La Net smiled, "Don't worry Logan couldn't feel it he is dead."

"I know but it makes me uncomfortable to think about cutting the penis like a fish," he replied adding. "How will that help prove that he had sex."

Dr. Fayette said, "I'll explain it this way. A bull dozer pushes dirt. It doesn't matter whether the dirt is wet or dry and how much resistance there is to the action. Dirt collects and sticks to the blade. The dozer operator stops periodically and violently shakes the blade to remove the dirt. During intercourse the penis is plowing, much like a dozer. Female secretions build up on the penis, under the foreskin and in the urethra. Sperm or other evidence may have collected inside the urethra tube. The tube extends further back into the body. If the male has an ejaculation, the urethra will be blown out; however some evidence may still remain."

A knock came at the office door. "Dr. Fayette the lab report just arrived" a voice called.

"Bring it in Ann"

La Net opened the report and looked at it for several minutes. "You two understand that more extensive testing will take at least two weeks. The toxicology report shows that Logan had a blood alcohol content of .06. Mr. Logan looks as if he was juiced up. He had traces of diazepam, ambien, and flunitarazepam which you likely know as rohypnol or GHB, the date rape drug in his system. It's a wonder that his respiratory system didn't collapse. I don't understand why he was bound. He couldn't move anyway with all that stuff in his body."

"Mr. Logan was kinky." She continued. "The swabs were analyzed. There was spermicidal gel in Logan's nasal passages, mouth, and throat, on his penis; and in his urethra tube. Sperm was detected in the penis swabs. It is not a regular test, but I asked the lab to run it. His sperm count was a hundred ninety thousand. He may have had sex but he didn't ejaculate. The count would be much lower if he had. So he went before he came, sorry, a little coroner humor."

She continued, "He was probably revived while whoever played games and tortured him. There were traces of ammonium nitrate in his nose, most likely smelling salts."

La Net paused, "What I don't know is what was in the needle. The drugs here are usually taken orally or slipped into a drink. The food that was not digested in Logan's stomach narrows the TOD to between 2:00AM and 7:00AM Monday."

Garbesi's cell phone chimed, playing the theme from the TV show *"Barney Miller"*. "Excuse me," he stood up and walked to a corner of the room.

He answered the phone, "Garbesi" the voice on the other end replied "this is George Calhoun; Lieutenant. I called the office, and Wood said to try your cell. Joe, are you close to a hard line? What I need to tell you should be on a secure line. You never know who has a scanner."

"I'm in Dr. Fayette's office."

George replied, "Good, she might want to hear this information."

La Net gave Calhoun her private number to bypass the receptionist. Minutes later, the phone rang.

"Calhoun you're on speaker phone Garbesi and Tyler are listening."

"Barbour's body was discovered Tuesday morning in a hotel in Richmond. His dick and balls were cut off." Calhoun said "Excuse me, ladies for my bluntness."

Liv looked at La Net and replied, "We know about these things continue."

"Detective Tucker Milliamp is working the case. Mr. Barbour was a vice president at a private bank. The bank has high profile clients with millions of dollars in deposits. A lady came into the bank on Monday morning, a real knockout looker. She said she was Morgan Roane and had IDs to prove it. She cashed the check from Logan's insurance company. According to Barbour's friend Barbour and Ms. Roane were going to lunch that afternoon."

La Net interrupted, "Detective this is Dr. Fayette; do you know who is doing the autopsy?"

"It is Dr. Steven Levine," replied Calhoun.

"Lieutenant, could you call Chief Summers and have him contact Richmond's Chief Jonas Bowles, so we could share information on these cases." Calhoun continued. "I would also like to stay here for the autopsy."

"George, I'll call Chief Summers as soon as we hang up."

"Joe, there are other similarities in the case. I will give the team a full report tonight or tomorrow."

They disconnected.

Joe asked "La Net, May I use your phone."

"Joe, use the phone in the next office. I want to call Dr. Levine and make some suggestions on what his office may want to look for in the autopsy."

Standing in the reception area, Joe pointed to a van outside the tinted windows. "Olivia do you see that van about half way down the block, the one that has ladders on top and a sign that says roofing on the side."

Tyler nodded positive.

"Yesterday the van said aluminum siding on the side. I noticed the dent on the rear quarter panel yesterday. The van has been following me since the press conference. I'm going to call the chief. Check to see if there are cameras on this building and try to get a license plate."

Tyler went to the car. When Joe got to the car, she offered him a hot dog.

"The cameras couldn't make out anything. I walked to the hot-dog vender and took a picture of the plate with my phone. It comes back to Todd Walker, a freelance writer. He sells to the highest bidder."

CHAPTER 9: FOLLOW-UP
THURSDAY MORNING

Thursday morning at 8:30AM Sgt. Tyler was prepping for the briefing. She had the dry- erase board up with all the updates on the case written on it. Lieutenant Garbesi was the last to arrive.

"Lieutenant, Chief Summers wants information for a press release by 10:00AM. I made copies of everything that's written on the board, and we can make notes on any new data."

Sgt. Tyler had written Logan and Barbour's names on the board, underlined them and drew a line between them. A list of comparisons was listed on the board between the two murder victims.

She addressed the room as soon as Garbesi was seated. "Detective Calhoun arrived back from Richmond late last night. Enough evidence has been collected in the murders of Upshur Logan and Doddridge Barbour. You can see from the comparisons that we and the Richmond Investigative Section found that the cases are related."

Tyler continued, "Composite drawings were made from descriptions that were given by the bartender, waitress, and other witnesses at the hotel. The drawings only varied slightly. Calhoun also brought a drawing from Richmond. The hotel clerk where the body was found gave a description of Barbour's companion. The only difference was the woman's hair which is red on the draw-ing Calhoun has. The other similarities are the removed testes, the wiped clean room, and the writing on the mirror."

"Dr. Fayette is working with Dr. Levine of Richmond, and autopsy results will be in later today. We have received answers from the admin messages we sent out. It appears that the other mysterious disappearances, deaths and murders of the men on Father McDowell's list may be related to our case and the Rich-mond case. Harrison is doing the follow-ups with other agencies. Valley Cove West Virginia doesn't have a teletype. We received a message from the West Virginia State Police Department that said we needed to contact the agency via phone. The sheriff in Valley Cove named Preston Scottsboro said the town records were in storage and we were welcome to come and search for a twenty plus year old record. I left the precinct phone number, e-mail address and mailing address if any other information could be obtained, with my name as contact. The sheriff did say he did not remem-ber much about Darla Knapper. He was young when she was sent away."

"I received an overnight package this morning that suggests that a secret is being kept in Valley Cove. The express envelope was postmarked from a town in Virginia that is twenty-five miles south of Valley Cove. Joe, after this briefing we can go over the contents in the envelope."

Sgt. Tyler pointed to the board, "We have three subs first, Darla Knapper which may be dead, Morgan Roane, I passed out the information I could find on her, and a mystery lady named Carla who was seen with Logan on the night before his body was found. They may all be the same woman or three different people."

Garbesi asked; "is there anything else to add?"

Calhoun said "Richmond PD pulled a videotape from the hotel parking lot. They were able to obtain a license number from the car, and a woman fitting our subject's description drove away in it. The car came back to a rental agency in Arlington. I gave the information to Harrison as soon as I had it."

Harrison spoke up. "The car was rented to Carla Hardy. We haven't been able to find any information on her."

"She had to have a credit card to rent a car" said the Lieutenant.

"She put down a thousand dollars cash deposit, and she had a driver's license from Illinois," said Harrison

"Let's, find out who this woman is" stated the Lieutenant.

"The FBI may get involved the money Roane put in the bank yesterday along with about ninety-nine million dollars has been moved from the Roane account. A million dollars was left in the account to keep it open and make it more difficult to detect right away," Sergeant Tyler reminded the detectives.

Garbesi asked, "Do we have any information on the Knapper woman?"

Harrison spoke up; "I received this late last night. I have contacted the West Virginia State Police. I spoke to a trooper in records. Ms. Knapper was committed for killing her stepfather in a domestic. The fire marshal declared the asylum fire set deliberately. The remains of the bodies were never identified conclusively; DNA testing wasn't as perfected in 2002 as it is now. They felt that the man was Jose Vasquez, a guard at the facility who was rumored and later confirmed to be raping Knapper and consensually having sex, with the second woman Morgan Roane. The state feels that Ms. Roane set the fire because she was committed for being a compulsive arsonist and to cover two murders. They believe Vasquez killed Knapper and Roane killed Vasquez after she saw what he had done."

Harrison continued "A letter was sent to the State Attorney General. It was post- marked the day after the fire. The letter outlined misconduct by the director on down to Vasquez. The director committed suicide when he found out about the investigation of his practices and behaviors. The records for Roane and Knapper were never recovered and were not backed up."

Garbesi asked, "Has father McDowell been excluded as a suspect?"

Tyler addressed all the detectives, "The Father's alibi has been checked out and he is excluded."

Garbesi adjourned the meeting telling "The detectives continue their follow ups."

Liv brought the express envelope delivered to the precinct earlier into the Joe's office. Joe, "I haven't looked at this yet. I was waiting for you.

"It is addressed to you, Olivia.

She opened the envelope and extracted two pieces of paper. One piece was typewritten and the second a carbon copy of a police report. The typewritten paper was transcribed.

Sgt. Tyler;

There are more secrets in Valley Cove than some of the people here know about.

Sometimes I think a blind eye is turned, so people can go on with their lives. If it

doesn't involve them, they don't want to get involved. Crimes have been covered

over the years to protect the guilty and scorn the innocent.

The police report on carbon was dated 1987. The copy was only of the front page of the report, which listed Darla Knapper as the complainant, along with her mother Colleen Knapper Mercer. The charges of forcible rape were printed on the sheet. Logan's and Barbour's names were visible as suspects. The copy appeared to be cut short. No more information was on it.

Garbesi sat for a minute with his hands folded in front of his mouth. Liv knew this was his thinking posture. "Tyler, "Do you think someone is trying to invite us for a visit?" Garbesi continued thinking out loud, "If we do find anything not dealing with our case we have to turn it over to the FBI. I will speak with the chief."

"Joe, you need to go now for your briefing with him."

After the briefing, Garbesi returned to Tyler's office, "Go pack a bag," he told her. "We're going to Valley Cove. I'll pick you up about 4:00PM. Sorry such short notice; the chief thought we needed to follow-up the letter. We'll stop and eat on the road. Everything in the town closes at 10:00PM."

CHAPTER 10:
VALLEY COVE, WEST VIRGINIA

Thursday afternoon, as they drove along I-66 westbound towards I-81 southbound, Tyler asked; "Joe, how did you get the chief to let us both go to Valley Cove?"

"I told him that the letter was addressed to you that this is a hot tip, and that Wood could run the investigation here for at least one day. The department is even going to spring for two hotel rooms, so we can get an early start. I gave the sheriff's office a heads up we are coming to look for the records. I didn't let them know about the letter. We can't be sure who sent it, but I bet it wasn't the sheriff. The chief said if we uncover any major wrong doing, we need to share information with the West Virginia State Police. We are just on a fact-finding mission pertaining to Logan and Barbour's murders."

The farther they drove from the city they noticed less and less houses and more and more open land and farms. Finally, they got to a point were they were driving over and coasting down rolling hills.

Joe looked at Liv, "We are almost to Valley Cove.

Liv slept most of the way and missed some beautiful scenery.

The sign for Valley Cove was read "WELCOME TO THE VILLAGE OF VALLEY COVE ESTABLISHED 1865." The town looked as if it had fallen off a 1950's post card. The buildings were old but well maintained. The most modern buildings were the sheriff's office, the jail and the court house, which were all in the same complex. The tallest building in the village was the Cove Hotel at four stories. Some of the roads were paved while others were still brick or cobblestone and only had two traffic lights.

Joe said, "Let's check in with the sheriff's office as a courtesy."

Joe pulled into a parking space. He and Tyler walked into the jail. It looked like a modern jail. There were four computer stations set up behind the front desk and a bullet- resistant glass wall with a sliding window set up in front.

Deputy Gilmer, spoke into an intercom, "May I help you."

"I am Lt. Garbesi, and this is Sgt. Tyler from Arlington Virginia.

The deputy hit a buzzer and spoke into the intercom, "Come in. I am Deputy Lewis Gilmer. Sheriff Scottsboro said, you would be coming in tonight. Do you want me to call him?"

"No. We can see him in the morning answered Garbesi. Deputy Gilmer may we ask you a couple of questions?"

"Anything Lieutenant to help your investigation; however I didn't know Darla Knapper. She was about six or seven years older than me. Knapper has two sisters and a mother living about two miles out of town. The people who might know more about the Knapper family are Abel and Yunis Frazil. They run the hotel and have lived here a long time and they are in their eighties."

Deputy, "Can we show you a sketch of a person of interest? See if you have ever scene her."

"Sgt. Tyler you can show me the picture. I hope I can help you.

Tyler showed Gilmer the sketches drawn from witness descriptions at the Logan and the Richmond hotel murder scenes.

Gilmer said, "He never scene her but she was sure pretty."

Sgt. Tyler slid the sketches back into her briefcase. "Thank you, Gilmer, Would you leave the sheriff a note that we will be in tomorrow?"

"Are we staying in the hotel across the street?" asked Garbesi.

"The sheriff reserved rooms for both of you," replied Gilmer.

Garbesi opened the door to the hotel. A brass bell was affixed to a catch at the top and rang as soon as the portal cleared it. The hotel was rustic to the early 1900s. The furniture had claw feet, and the sofa and chairs appeared to be antiques with covers on them to save the upholstery. The registration desk was made of mahogany, and a little old balding white man with a few age spots on his forehead was sitting behind it.

"Welcome to the Valley Cove Hotel, detectives. "My name is Abel Frazil, I'm the proprietor. Lewis called and said you were on the way over."

"What else did Lewis tell you?" Garbesi asked in a disgusted voice?

Abel spoke in an old man's crackly voice as if he was upset,

"Lieutenant, don't get your panties in an uproar. This is a small county; everyone knows everyone and you can't keep secrets in this town."

"I apologize, Mr. Frazil for my ignorance," said Garbesi.

"Please detectives," call me Abel. Abel spoke in a calmer voice. "Lewis told me you wanted to know about the Knapper family, Darla in particular and show me a picture." Abel, began I need to give you some back ground first. Valley Cove was once classified as a city. We had a population of over thirty thousand and the county numbered at fifty thousand. Coal was big in the 1950s and if you were not educated, unskilled, or couldn't get a job for any reason. You could come here and get employment."

"Sheriff Hancock, which was Scottsboro's great-uncle, liked the money and taxes being brought into the town but did not care for the as he termed it different people. He was a bigot. Everyone who wasn't white had to live in the county outside city limits. The Hancock family owned everything, so it was easy for them to regulate prices and would artificially bump prices on land, housing, food, and anything else they could without raising suspicion from the feds. They also ran the local government. Darla's, daddy Drew Knapper, and his family were the first niggros to live in town. I'm sorry Niggros isn't a proper word. I don't like that slang word they use for black people and colored people isn't right."

Able said "Forgive me for rambling. Drew's daddy, Boone was a WWII and Korean War vet and still had contacts in Washington. The sheriff and the city council were pissed when the Knapper family moved to town but they couldn't do anything about it. Drew went off to the Vietnam War and was a hero. His daddy died in a coal mine accident while he was gone overseas. The accident was termed 'suspicious.' The investigation was inclusive. Boone's wife died shortly after that of a heart attack."

"Hancock thought he got rid of the Knapper family. Drew was discharged at the end of the conflict and came back to close out the homestead and his parents affairs. Drew was going to move out of the area. He started dating a local girl, Colleen Pendleton. She got pregnant with Darla. The sheriff was infuriated that a black man had gotten a white woman pregnant.

Drew married Colleen, and they bought a place outside town. Drew went to work in the mines. The problems with Drew and the sheriff continued."

"You see the gas station down the road? I owned it before a big company came by and put in a Quick Snax and Gas. Three fellows two white, and one black came to town in the 70s to sell or buy drugs. They did not get anything and decided to rob me at the station. They didn't want to leave town empty-handed. I couldn't open the safe. I was nervous. The fellows started to beat me into unconsciousness. People drove past, but Drew stopped and beat all three of them down. When I awoke in the hospital three days later, my wife told me that the four men who'd done this were arrested. Three of them were hospitalized with guards. I told her there were only three. Drew saved my life. The sheriff said the drugs had me messed up, and I was talking out of my head. Drew had money in his pocket and some kind of belt in martial arts. Drew was a dangerous weapon and needed to be behind bars. I told my wife to call the state's attorney from a phone out of the area."

"The next day not only was the West Virginia State's attorney at my bed but the US District Attorney was by his side. They let Drew go with a full apology. I found out that after hearing my story the US District Attorney ordered his release. I was told that he told the sheriff that, if he did not let Drew out and drop the charges. The FBI would have fifty agents come to town and climb up his and the city council's ass with a microscope. I think Drew made a call because my wife said she didn't."

"Drew died in a coal mine accident when Darla was about five years old. The investigation was termed inclusive. Colleen and Darla lived on the property outside town."

"When Darla was about eight years old Colleen married Clay Mercer Sr., an alcoholic piece of garbage. He was just like his daddy, no good. I think Colleen was lonely and thought that Darla needed a father figure."

"Darla's Godfather Burrell Holmes. His last name is spelled H-O-L-M-E-S. The H is silent. Holmes was a state police man when Darla killed Mercer. She turned herself into him. Darla was afraid of the sheriff Hancock."

"How long was Hancock sheriff?" asked Tyler.

"The sheriff's office has always been in the Hancock family. The term limits prevent them from running more than two consecutive times, a term is four years. A relative runs for office for two terms and then they come back for two more terms. The Hancock family, along with my family, was part of the original settlers in this valley. The Hancock that was in office at the time was the son of the sheriff who had it in for the Knapper family. He carried his daddy's angers and prejudices with him. I think his father was still running the department."

"Things have changed around here with Sheriff Scottsboro. His mother is a Hancock, but he is the sheriff. He married Holmes's daughter about seven years ago. Most of the Hancock family will not speak to him for marring a black woman. The younger Hancock generation is all right with it."

A feminine voice came from behind the curtain. "Grandpa, Mamma wants you to come watch the eleven o'clock news with her."

A girl of about twenty-one entered the room. "Excuse me, I heard the bell but I thought our guests had gone upstairs already."

Abel introduced her as Joan his granddaughter.

"Can you look at these sketches before you leave?" Tyler asked Abel.

Abel and Joan looked at the pictures. Joan spoke first "Never seen her."

Able studied the sketches for a minute. "They look like the same woman high cheek bones, same size nose and nostrils, and full lips. The hair is a different style and color. She is very lovely, and it could be Darla if she was alive."

Abel stood up with his cane and started to walk through the curtain. Abel paused, "You might want to talk to Holmes," And he disappeared behind the cloth.

Garbesi spoke up, "I hope we didn't upset your grandfather."

Joan looked at the two detectives, "No Grandpa has an eye for details, and pretty girls and he likes to talk. He doesn't miss an episode of the forensic files, and cold case files intrigue him."

"Joan, where is a good place for have breakfast?" asked Garbesi.

"The Cove Café is the only place in town for breakfast, unless you want a computer- generated, fake egg bagel from the gas station. I didn't know Darla but her half sister, Virginia Mercer is a waitress at the cafe. She seems to be a nice person. She keeps to herself and doesn't socialize with people in town too much." Joan handed them keys to rooms 201 and 203.

The next morning, Garbesi and Tyler met in the hotel lobby to go to breakfast. An older silver haired woman looked up from behind the registration desk; "Good morning." "I am Yunis Abel's wife."

The detectives said, "Good morning" in unison.

Tyler added, "I hope we didn't keep your husband up too late."

"No, we saw the news. I didn't know Darla. I think a good person to talk with is Mr. Holmes. Speak with his daughter first, the sheriff's wife. Holmes don't care for outsiders."

"Thank you for the information, Yunis. Could you look at the sketches to see if you recognize the woman in them?" asked Tyler.

Yunis spoke, "I don't see well anymore, and have had trouble with memory as of late."

"Thank you anyway, we are going for breakfast."

"Will you be staying tonight detectives? Yunis inquired.

"I don't think so. We will be back later to settle our bill and make a decision," said Garbesi.

At the Café, the detectives glanced at the menu and noticed people all of whom were staring at them.

The waitress came over and spoke "Don't pay any attention to them. Everyone knows why you're here and wonders if you're going to ask them any questions. I'm Virginia. I will be on break in a half hour. Meet me at the back door and we will talk. Would you like to order now?"

They both ordered coffee and the cove breakfast. They finished, paid the bill, and left a nice tip. Then, they headed towards the rear door of the café. Virginia let them in to the manager's office.

Virginia spoke first, "I don't want to air dirty or clean laundry in the public. Everyone in this town knows everyone's business. I try to stay to myself and take care of my family. I have two conditions. I will tell you what I know, if you agree to them."

"May we hear your conditions first?" queried the detectives.

"You can not bother my mother or my little sister. My stepmother who has been a mother to me for years is not well. She became an alcoholic when my father died and Darla was sent away for it. She had a nervous breakdown when we were told that Darla

67

died in the fire. I take care of her. Michele who is my half sister, Colleen and Clay's daughter is a med student on a scholarship at WVU and was too young to remember anything."

Garbesi and Tyler said, "We will agree to your conditions."

Virginia continued, "Clay, my father, was a fucking tyrant and an alcoholic. I believe that he killed my real mother. I was told she committed suicide. If she did it was to escape the beatings and rape of that sadistic bastard. I was a year older than Darla when Colleen married Clay. I thought that he had changed because he didn't touch me after he married her at least for about a year. When Colleen became pregnant, with Michele that all changed. The bastard was sneaking back into my room at night and doing things that a father shouldn't do. He told me that if I said anything to anyone he would kill Darla, Colleen, the baby, and me."

"I don't know if he ever took Darla. I do know about the Darla rape and that Clay wouldn't let her report it. Clay kept referring to Darla as damaged goods. Mom and Darla did try to report it, but it was a week after the rape happened."

"The night Clay died he was in a drunken stupor. He went after Michele, she was six years old. Darla hit him in the head with a shovel several times."

Garbesi interrupted, "She was defending someone else who could not defend themselves? Why was she convicted?"

Virginia continued, "She wasn't. She was sent away to an institution because of the history with the Knapper family and the Hancock family. Holmes believed she would be safe. I thought it was a private school. I didn't know that it was a mental asylum."

Tyler pulls the sketches from her briefcase and asked, "Virginia, to see if she recognized the woman in the picture."

Virginia looked at the sketches. "The woman in these pictures is very beautiful. I don't recognize her."

Tyler said, "A couple more questions please."

"Okay, I need to get back to work."

"Do you know of anyone who would want to get revenge on Darla's behalf for the rape," inquired Tyler.

"I want you to know that Darla was liked by everyone," Virginia said. "She was a kindhearted person. I take care of my mom and have a sitter while at work. Michele lives over on the Monongalia River during the year while attending school in Morgantown."

"You aren't suspects," said Garbesi.

"I just wanted you to know where Michele and I were during the murders you are investigating." "I think you need to talk with Trooper Holmes."

Garbesi asked; "Did you send the letter to Olivia to bring us here?"

"Someone gave it to Yunis. She gave it to me. She knew that I am one of the only people who can leave town undetected. I don't know what was in it and don't want to know. I did a favor for a friend. I need to get back to work now."

The detectives walked to the jail, where they were greeted by the receptionist Ms. Adeline Wyoming. "Good morning Lieutenant, good morning Sergeant. The sheriff has been waiting for you. Call me Addie. I have been the receptionist at this department for forty three years. I will be helping you locate the records you seek, if they exist."

Addie was a lady of about seventy years, with white hair, who looked as if she maintained her shape and youthful appearance and kept a pleasant attitude. "Let me introduce you to Sheriff Scottsboro." She led the detectives to an office at the rear of the station and knocked on a door. "Detectives Garbesi and Tyler from Arlington County are here to see you."

"Send them in, Addie I will call you when we're done."

Sheriff Scottsboro was a young man of about thirty years old. He stood around six foot one inch" and weighed in at two hundred fifteen pounds. His build was lean, and hair was cut in a military fashion, off the ears, the neck and close to the scalp. "Welcome to our county," he said.

After greetings and handshakes the sheriff offered the detectives a seat. "I apologize for not being here when you arrived last night." The sheriff continued, "As you probably have found out by now everyone in town knows or has some idea why you to are here. When your teletype came over the wire to the West Virginia State Police, people in town knew before I did. They started asking me questions, and I had no idea what they were talking about. Ever since I was a little boy, I always wondered where the network of communication started in the community. It may be one of those mysteries never solved."

Garbesi said, "May I ask you a question, sheriff?"

"Go ahead."

"No disrespect intended, how long have you been sheriff?"

"I anticipated that question, I am thirty years old. I spent eight years in the army as military police. I was stationed in the Middle Eastern theater of operations, in Germany, South Korea, and Central America. I left the service as a captain because I was needed at home for an ill father. I was elected sheriff about eight months ago. Since, I became sheriff. The department has started to move forward. We have installed new computers and are beginning to back up all of our old case files. The previous administrations, which I am sorry to say, were all relatives have had blemishes of corruption. I am trying to clean the department's image with the state and feds."

"When I was young, I noticed laws were being broken and who was doing it. I noticed people related to officials in the town and county getting away with crimes and people who were considered outsiders being persecuted. This office is a satellite office. The county seat is ten miles away and that is the main station."

Garbesi apologized; "I did not mean to question your ability or credentials. We are not here to investigate you or your department."

Scottsboro replied, "I did not mean to sound curt. I have been answering that question since I was elected, and answering for my predecessor's faults."

"We found this file on the Knapper/Mercer murder. It is limited. I am waiting for clearance from the West Virginia States Attorney to release a copy to you. It shouldn't be a problem because it is not an active case. You can look it over if you desire. The state police made the arrest and the file they have is more detailed."

"The alleged rape of Ms. Knapper is a mystery. I heard about it. I was only eight or nine years old at the time. I can't locate a record of it being reported. You are welcome to look through the old files but I can't say it happened because I don't know. Addie will assist you in whatever you need."

Scottsboro said, "Gilmer told me you have sketches. May I see the drawings you have?"

Tyler pulled the drawing from her briefcase.

Scottsboro studied them, "She looks familiar but I can't say that I have seen her around here. I knew of Darla. I saw her around school. She was probably five years older then me."

"The name of Burrell Holmes keeps coming up," said Sgt. Tyler. "Can you tell us about him?"

"He is my father in-law. My wife Neosha is bringing me lunch in a couple hours and she can tell you about her father."

Scottsboro pushed the intercom switch; "Addie will you come in please."

Addie appeared at the door seconds later.

"May I use a telephone, Sheriff?" asked Garbesi. The cell doesn't seem to have a signal here."

"Addie will show you a secured line."

"Liv, I'm going to check in with Wood to see if anything new has been discovered in our investigation. You work with Ms. Addie to see if you can locate anything."

Garbesi was on the phone with Wood for more than an hour.

When he was finished, Liv and Addie came back from the cellar. "We couldn't find any new files Joe. Did Wood have anything new?"

Scottsboro, came into the room "pardon me detectives, Neosha came to town early. Do you want to speak with her about her father?"

Addie shows the detectives to an interrogation room for privacy.

Neosha was a petit woman of five foot five inches with medium brown skin, high cheek bones, long plaited hair and a smile that could brighten any room.

"Preston tells me that you are looking into the Darla Knapper case," she said. "The case has been closed for years and I am not sure that my father can tell you anything. I do know that he is, or was, Darla's godfather. Darla was a few years older than me and like my big sister. I did not see her much after her mother married Mercer.

I know that Darla called my father the night Mercer died, because she did not trust anyone else."

"My father lives alone and has many friends that are not quite human. He doesn't like strangers and is different from anyone you will ever meet. We get along fine. I think his estranged behavior toward others come from his days working for the federal government. He lives on Doctarie Lane about four miles up Route 460. I will call to let him know you are coming if you want to go up."

"We would like to speak with him," Garbesi stated. "We can be there about 3:00 pm. Thank you, Ms. Scottsboro for your time." "Liv let's go to lunch."

On the way to lunch walking down the street, Garbesi spoke to Liv. "Wood tells me that the gang unit believes that the numbers on the mirror that looked like a fraction most likely represents kills versus how many are left on the list that McDowell gave us. The section has received several reports back from other jurisdictions and the first number is different while last number is always thirteen. The stick symbol on the mirror appears to be some kind of hieroglyphic insect. The drugs used in the murders varied but produced similar effects in the victims. The sketches from witnesses all appear similar with slight variations. All the scenes were wiped clean and most of the cases have been placed in the cold files. McDowell has accepted limited protection. Our guys are not allowed in the church with guns. Taylor thinks it is bullshit and asked to be left alone."

"Joe," Olivia whispered, "I have some information. I'll tell you on the way to Holmes's place."

Liv spoke to Garbesi in the car. "Addie told me about the rape case. I did not tell you in the café because I didn't want anyone to hear us. Addie gave me the information in confidence."

Addie said that Scottsboro is a good man, and he is beginning to understand the corruption and malfeasances that his ancestors have brought about over the years. He is trying to correct them. Addie was working the day that Darla and her mother came to report the rape. Mercer, the stepfather made Darla's mother burn all the clothes she wore that night. However, Colleen saved Darla's underwear and placed them in a plastic bag."

"The deputy who took the report died about ten years ago. The crime was reported a week after it allegedly happened. The detectives would write the reports and then Addie had to type it with carbon paper between three sheets of paper. They used a machine called a ditto for extra copies if they needed more copies."

"Two of the boys named as alleged perps in the rape were Sheriff Hancock's grandsons. The Hancock brothers were on McDowell's list. The older one, Mason, went missing several months after the incident and his brother, Grant, was murdered a few years ago. An investigation into the rape allegations lasted maybe three days and the sheriff declared it a waste of time, there was no evidence, no one to validate the story, and no one would come forward with information. The rape kit showed that Darla was torn vaginally and anally, but the sheriff declared it consensual, even though the doctor and nurses did not feel the same."

"Addie was ordered to destroy all records and anything pertaining to the case, since everyone involved was under eighteen years old. Addie saved a copy of the report. She said that she felt it might come back to bite the department someday. Plus, the sheriff ordered the destruction not the states attorney's office; which is not legal in West Virginia. She said that it was the only copy she knew of. However Hancock did allot of crooked stuff and may have saved a copy to blackmail his grandsons if they did not do what he wanted."

"The package was left on here desk and instruction were given to her to make sure that it got to us."

CHAPTER 11: DOCTARIE LANE, HOLMES'S PLACE

"Joe, the lane is on the left. If we go too fast, Neosha said, we'll miss it. The lane is hidden in the woods."

Joe slowed to make the turn. "Did you know, Liv, that Doctarie is a Swahili word meaning doctor?"

They entered the lane and came upon a gate. The gate had a sign posted on it: "DO NOT ENTER". A skull and cross bones was scribed as a warning below the words.

Liv looked at Joe, "I am not sure about this."

"Neosha said she would let her dad know we are coming, Olivia." Joe said, "I'll open the gate. Drive the car through then I'll close it."

Liv drove the car through and moved to the passenger seat. Joe slid back into the driver's seat. One hundred yards down the lane, the main road disappeared from sight. A second sign had written on it "TURN AROUND NOW" the car inched farther up the road. Fifty more yards down the road one more sign was posted with the words "LAST CHANCE"; there was a cut in the road large enough for a tractor to turn around.

Joe asked Liv, "Do you want to turn around?"

"Joe, we are almost to Holmes's house," Said Tyler.

"Liv, I need to tell you, when I opened the gate, a surveillance system of some kind was activated. I heard a click and saw a motion detector in the trees. We have been tracked since we entered the property."

The detectives pulled into a clearing about a hundred yards from the house. A thunderous voice came booming from the trees: "Stop the car and turn off the engine."

When the car had stopped, two German shepherds dogs flanked both driver's and passenger's doors at fifty feet away.

The voice boomed again, "Follow my instructions and everything will be all right. Driver and passenger, roll down your windows and stick your hands outside the car."

"I have been trying to stop cursing, Joe, but is he pulling a fucking felony traffic stop on us."

"Liv just do what he says, Neosha told us he was different. We can't see him, but he sees us, and the dogs have his cover."

They complied and put their hands out the windows.

The tree voice said, "Driver, with your left hand, remove the ignition key, and drop, it out the window, now."

Garbesi did as the voice commanded.

"Driver exit, the vehicle and keep your hands in the air. Passenger, keep your hands out the window. Driver, step away from the car. With your left thumb and forefinger remove the weapon from your holster drop the magazine to the ground, lock the slide back and place it on the ground in front of you. Step away from the weapon."

The voice spoke in a foreign language and the dog in front of Garbesi approached him sniffed around him and returned to a sitting position in his original spot.

"Passenger, I want you to do the exact same thing," the voice commanded.

Olivia complied. The dog on her side of the car was given the same instructions as Garbesi's guard. The dog on Olivia's flank sat on her side. The voice commanded, "Passenger, remove the gun from your ankle holster." Tyler followed the instructions, and the dog returned to its post.

A large black man standing about six foot two inches emerged from the shadow of trees carrying a desert eagle 50 caliber handgun pointed at his visitors and a high-powered rifle slung over his shoulder.

Joe spoke, 'Mr. Holmes you can put that away."

"I don't do wet work for the government any more" Holmes expressed.

"We are not here for that. We talked with your daughter. She was supposed to call you and let you know we were coming up. I'm Joe Garbesi and my partner is Olivia Tyler. We are detectives from Virginia."

Holmes, put the weapon in his shoulder clutch. "Please, put your hands down and show me your credentials. I have been out all day and may have missed Neosha's call, my name is Burrell." He turned to the dogs and called them by name "Harley, Mullah." Holmes gave them a command in the language, he was using before. The dogs ran back to the house and posted themselves on each side of the porch steps as if they were sentries.

Tyler asked; "What language are you speaking?"

"I give the dogs instructions in German." Holmes invited them to the house. "Put your weapons in the car. The dogs don't let anyone enter the house but me with guns."

The detectives secured their weapons in the car and started to walk to the house with Holmes. Tyler froze in her tracks, and Garbesi almost fell over her.

Garbesi said; "Liv what are you doing?"

Liv stopped and pointed at a black bear coming up the field from the lake with a fish in his mouth, "B...bear," She stuttered.

Holmes moved close to her and said in a calm voice "watch this."

The bear ran up to the porch not bothering the dogs. He put the fish down and appeared to cut it with his claws. He moved away, and three kittens and a momma cat came from under the porch and started eating the lake trout. The bear went back to the lake and returned with his own dinner. He sat down in the corner where the porch meets the house and ate his fish.

Tyler looked at Holmes in wonderment. "Did he just feed those cats?"

"Yes, the cats used to steal his food, and I guess he got tired of it, and now he catches two at a time. The bear's name is Dory Funk Jr."

"Mr. Holmes is he one of your pets?" asked Tyler.

"No ma'am, I think he thinks I am his pet. I live here, and the animals live here, we co-exist and it works out. Let's go to the house."

As they approached the steps, the bear looked up. Holmes, directed a statement towards the bear in Spanish, and Dory went back to eating. "I told him it was alright. You are friends."

They entered the house, a modest single-level hovel with a clean, well setup kitchen, and living room area with a brick fireplace. A den was off to the side of the living room. Holmes put the rifle in the corner of the living room, walked to the kitchen washed his hands, and turned on the coffee maker.

Garbesi asked, "Why all the security? I noticed when I opened the gate that a sensor was triggered."

Holmes answered; "Have you ever heard of William Pierce, the author of the *Tipper Diaries* a book about white supremacy. He passed years ago, but there are still people in this area who believe it is not right for a black man to own five hundred acres of land. I still get harassed occasionally. Poachers are also a problem in this area. They will kill animals and harvest their organs. The organs are sold for medicines and aphrodisiacs to foreign buyers. It's big money. The poachers will leave the carcasses lying around the land to rot, which is how I came upon Dory Funk. A couple years ago, before I installed the entire security system, there were some buzzards circling a couple miles north of here. I went up with the dogs to search around the area. I thought the poachers were back."

"The mother bear had been shot and gutted. The cub was trying to protect her body from predators. It took an hour before I could gain his trust and convince him that the dogs did not want to eat his momma's body. The cub was convinced, when a wolf tried to attack and the dogs chased it away. I buried her on the mountain and raised the cub. The bear and the dogs became good friends. When the bear got too big to stay in the house, I build him a hooch similar to a cave with a gate in the backyard. I released him on the mountain around the area where he was found. He kept coming back to sleep in his crib. One day, I was looking for Mae the mother cat. She was pregnant at the time. I realize a bear can be a dangerous animal and had thought that maybe he finally got mad with her for taking his food. I found the cat in his cave. She delivered the three kittens, and he acted like a surrogate father protecting them. He thinks they are family."

"The security comforts me. I like to know who is on the property. Let me go wash up while the coffee is brewing. The cups are above the sink." Holmes disappeared into a back room.

Garbesi and Tyler looked at the pictures on the fireplace mantel, pictures of Scottsboro, Neosha and their two children, a pretty woman who looked like Neosha's mother; the dogs with the children and Holmes in an army uniform with some of his buddies. A shadow box hung on the wall containing two Silver Stars, a Bronze Star and two Purple Heart medals.

Holmes came out of the back room with a towel wiping his hands. "I know the two of you didn't come all the way from Arlington to talk about the animals or poaching, and you are not from Langley, Virginia. How can I help you?" asked Holmes.

Garbesi started to tell the story of the murdered people who were allegedly involved in the brutal rape of Darla twenty plus years ago, and how, Berkley McDowell approached them with the theory of a serial killer out for revenge for Darla.

Tyler continued "There have been two murders one in Arlington and one in Richmond within a couple days of each other. Both men were on the McDowell list naming them as being involved with the rape. Two names are still on the list, and McDowell is scared."

Holmes pondered a thought; "You don't believe this is a coincidence?"

The detectives both said "No."

Holmes pointed to the army picture on the mantel, that showed Darla's father, Drew. He then pointed to the medals in the shadow box. "Drew had twice as many. We promised each other, that if one of us died. The other would take care of his family. I tried to take care of Darla and her mother. When Drew died, Darla would come up here every day. I taught her the basics about life and how to survive in the world. Darla, Neosha and I practiced martial arts. I made sure their schoolwork was done. They both learned to speak Spanish. Six months after Mercer married Darla's, mother the visits stopped. Darla would call me every once in awhile. She told me that Mercer thought that it wasn't right for a young pretty girl, to spend so much time with an older man and a nigger at that even if she was half nigger herself. The fact that he called me a nigger did not bother me. Ignorant people use that word. What bothered me is that he would insinuate that I might be attempting to influence or do unnatural things with a child."

"The son of a bitch was uneducated and ignorant anyway. We as a society deal with them everyday. Darla told me about the rape six weeks after it happened. When I tried to investigate it, all the evidence had been destroyed. Hancock told me to keep my nose out of town business. The case was closed. I believed she was raped. I couldn't prove it."

The night Darla called me; "she did not say much. She wanted me to come in uniform and my State Police car to the old Brinson Mine. She did not want to discuss it on the phone. She said she was in trouble. When I arrived, I found Mercer dead with his skull bashed in on the back of the pickup truck. Darla said, she did it to protect her baby sister. She called me because of how the sheriff had treated her in the past. I did a thorough investigation, and it was determined that Darla was defending someone who could not defend themselves."

"The state also looked into Darla's background and determined that she had psychological problems from incidents that happened prior to the murder and ordered her to a state institution Poca-hontas/Pendleton State Hospital, for evaluation. I didn't have any-thing to do with her being sent away. I was glad she was going away from this area. She asked me after the trial to make sure her sisters and mother stayed together."

Tyler asked; "Do you think that anyone would want to get revenge for Darla?"

Holmes answered, "I did, but it is one thing to think about it and another to act on it. Besides if I did it not you nor anyone else, would never know. I was in federal court in Kentucky testifying in an animal poaching case for the last two weeks."

Holmes wrote his name and phone number on a piece of paper, "This is my secured line if you need anything else."

One more question said Tyler; "Do you think Darla is still alive."

Holmes thought for a moment, "Anything is possible. She hasn't contacted me, and the last time I saw her was two months before the hospital fire."

Just then an alarm went off in the house. A red light the size of a button was flashing and making a loud beeping sound.

Tyler startled; "What's that alarm?"

"Someone has breached the perimeter," Holmes replied calmly. "You can call if you need anything else. I will turn off the alarm on the gate you came in, and you can show yourselves out." Holmes opened his laptop and started punching keys.

Garbesi asked; "Do you need any help?"

Holmes said, "It's my problem not yours."

"I think we'll wait to leave" expressed Garbesi.

Holmes pulled up a schematic of the alarm system. "The breach is at the northwest quad, Delta 1, 2, and 3 cameras are active." Holmes added, "As long as the two of you insist on staying you can make yourselves useful." He pushed a hidden button and the fireplace mantel moved. Behind the mantel was a room full of computer equipment that looked as if it had come from the Pentagon. The room had a large screen on the wall showing the plat of Holmes's property. Lights were blinking at the breach points. Holmes tapped a couple of keys on the console and silenced the alarm. A smaller TV screen on the console focused on the positions where the cameras had been set off. A silver Range Rover came into sight, and three heat signatures were detected within.

Holmes pointed to the screen, "There are three people in the vehicle. We can't see in because the windows are tinted. We can close in on the license plates. I need to go out there. You two stay here in the house for your safety, until I come back."

Garbesi asked; "Do you need back up? I am volunteering."

"If you go with me, you have to follow my directions to the letter." Holmes pressed another button, and a wall opened revealing a variety of weapons and bulletproof vests. "Joe put this on. I can't have people crawling all over this mountain if something happens to you. You can use the rifle by the door in the living room, and take this sig 9mm for a backup."

Holmes took a 12-gauge pump shotgun from the wall and put the desert eagle in the holster.

Tyler asked; "What can I do?"

"Watch the monitor and call my son-in-law. His private number is by the phone; tell him we have possible poachers, at least three. Give him the information on the vehicle and tell him to use the buffalo trail gate on the north." Holmes tuned the radio on the console to a frequency. This is your way to communicate with us. We will each have ear- pieces tuned to the same frequency. If something changes with those clowns, tell us. Just use our names. No one else can pick up the radio communications. Please, stay in the house. The animals may be spooked if you go out and I'm not here."

Garbesi and Holmes walked from the house. Holmes turned and said something to the dogs in German, the bear in Spanish and the cats in English. "I told the dogs to watch the house and the bear to watch the dogs, cats, and house." Holmes went inside the garage, as the door opened, a camouflaged hummer emerged. "Stand outside the vehicle for a minute and don't be alarmed. The dogs need to get your scent."

Holmes went back into the garage and Garbesi noticed written on the back wall, "Home of the Minnesota Wrecking Crew, Enter at your own risk."

Two of the largest dogs Garbesi ever had ever seen emerged from the garage. They circled Garbesi, sniffed, and when they were satisfied they sat on each side of him.

"They trust you and have your scent," Holmes expressed.

Garbesi said, "Thank goodness, I won't want to meet them in an alley."

Holmes laughed, "They are big babies," He said and as he knelt beside them. They lapped his face. Holmes explained "they're Anatoli Shepherds dogs" as he hooked collars on each of them. He gave them instructions in Italian, and they ran out in front of the hummer and up the path.

"You told them to find the bad guys," My Italian is rusty. "When I was a child my mother taught me," Garbesi explained.

The two men got into the hummer and Holmes opened the glove compartment. "The yellow indicators are the dogs, Charlie 1 is Gene, and Charlie 2 is Ole. The red light in front is the target vehicle. If the car is moving it will start blinking. The vehicle is stationary now." Holmes checked the head set, "Tyler, can you hear me?"

"Yes, loud and clear,' Tyler came back over the headset.

Garbesi then tried. The commo was clear.

The hummer came to a stop three hundred yards from the target vehicle. Holmes asked Garbesi, "Where are the dogs?"

"They split up by the thickets Gene is going east and Ole is going west," answered Garbesi.

Holmes said "They are circling the vehicle. I want you to go in the wood line about ten yards and you will see a ridge. You can see everything in the rifle scope. I don't want you involved anymore than necessary. Just watch my back and talk to me if you see anything out of the ordinary."

Holmes shook Garbesi's hand and told him "to be careful."

Garbesi makes it to the ridge, and speaks into the throat mike, "Holmes; I see three subjects. The driver is a blonde guy. A red headed fellow got out of the passenger side. They both have weapons in shoulder holsters. The third guy is bald; he is in the back of the vehicle. I can't see if he is armed. I see Ole; he is lying in the wood line behind baldy."

Holmes pumped the shotgun and stopped the hummer at an angle fifteen yards from the Range Rover. He got out and hid the shotgun behind his leg. Holmes spoke, "This is private property, no trespassing. I have to ask you to leave."

The blonde guy spoke. "We missed the turn on the road and crashed through the fence," the blond guy replied. Blondey and Red turned to get in the vehicle. Blondey turned, "I think we want to stay."

Holmes raised the shotgun. "I don't want any violence. The sheriff will be here soon, and I will not press charges if you leave now."

Baldy came out from behind the vehicle with a FN FAL (Model 50) .280-rifle with a scope attached to it. Blondey spoke, "Mr. Holmes put down your weapon."

What the hell this asshole was doing with a Belgium made weapon? Garbesi thought.

He could hear everything in his earbud and was taking aim with the high-powered rifle at Baldy when he felt a steel muzzle of an M16 on his cheek. A man with a cowboy hat was standing above Garbesi, "Leave the rifle on the ground and get up slow."

Garbesi spoke softly into his throat mike "they got me Holmes."

A crackle came from a hand held radio in the Range Rover, "Stephen, I have a second guy on the ridge with a rifle. I'm bringing him down."

Blondey directed comments at Holmes, "We should have a good pay day. Our white friends on the other side of the mountain have put a fifty thousand dollar bounty on your life but we aren't going to kill you. We'll just deliver you to them. Mr. Holmes, we have your friend. Put the gun down, and take off the shoulder holster."

Holmes complied.

Cowboy Hat gave Garbesi instructions; "Put your hands on your head" Cowboy moved up and took the pistol from Garbesi and shoved it in his waistband, then stooped and picked up the rifle. "Straight done the hill and join your friend."

Cowboy Hat was about three yards behind Garbesi on the path and not in eyeshot of the other bad guys when the Anatoli

Shepherd took him by surprise. Gene was on top of Cowboy Hat before he could say a thing into his walkie-talkie.

Garbesi spoke calmly in bad Italian. The dog must have understood to get off the cowboy because Gene backed up and stood guard over the fallen captor. Garbesi spoke softly into his throat mike, "Holmes, I'm clear."

It was like the dogs had coordinated their attack. At the same time Gene attacked cowboy, Ole took out Baldy and the FN FAL, which gave Holmes enough time to take out Red with a leg sweep and pick up the shotgun and point it at Blondey's melon. Garbesi got to the vehicle with Cowboy. He and Holmes held the four subjects until the sheriff arrived.

Holmes sent the dogs home. Scottsboro looked in a cooler in the back of the Range Rover and found harvested organs from different types of wildlife.

Scottsboro looked at Holmes. "Neosha worries about you up here by yourself."

Holmes responded, "You know son, my new friend Joe saved my life and has made me look at people differently. Tell my daughter I'm fine. Bring the kids and come up for a cookout this weekend."

Scottsboro turned to Garbesi, and said "I need you to come to the station to make a statement."

Joe nodded in agreement.

"Sheriff, I will be at the station in about a half hour to file the complaint. I need to show my guest out explained Holmes.

When Holmes and Garbesi arrived back at the house, Liv was sitting on the porch with the kittens in her lap, the momma cat at her feet, the dogs on post, and the bear in the corner. Holmes looked at her in amazement.

Liv said, "I gained the trust of the bear by speaking to him in Spanish, and the dogs and cats followed his lead. I am sorry. I didn't see the fourth guy until it was too late. They dropped him off when they came through the fence." Liv continued, "I reviewed the tapes."

Joe looked at Liv, "We need to stay tonight. The sheriff needs me to make a statement. We can stay at Cove Hotel again tonight. We'll leave for Arlington in the morning."

Holmes, spoke, "Before you leave I have a picture of Darla. She was fifteen year old at the time. It was taken before she was sent away. I would like to get it back. What those boys did to her wasn't right. I actually hope you have luck, but I think those boys have destroyed so many lives and ran free for years. I can't cry for them."

Liv and Garbesi drove out the road toward the highway. "Joe, what do you think about Holmes?"

"I am glad he is on our side," Garbesi replied. "I think Holmes is a combination of the beast master, 007 and Robocop. I think he has been honest with us."

Liv said, "I do too."

"I will go to write the statement at the sheriff's office. Liv, go get some rest. You can drive first in the morning."

CHAPTER 12:
THE ABDUCTION

The detectives pulled into Arlington at around 1:00 PM Saturday.

"I am going to the office Liv; do you want dropped at home? I need to add the information into the murder investigation book and to see if any new information was uncovered."

Joe, "I will go in with you."

"I promise we will only be there for an hour or two," replied Joe.

They pulled into the station and noticed all the detective's cars parked in the lot. Thinking out loud Tyler said, "I wonder what's going on at the office all these cars on a Saturday."

Wood met the detectives at the door. "I tried to call this morning. The sheriff told me you had left already." I will explain everything, "McDowell and Taylor are missing." The coffee is fresh, and I'll be in the conference room."

Garbesi and Tyler grab a cup of coffee and move to the conference room.

Wood began, ""Joe after I talked to you yesterday, I received a phone call from the missing persons unit at about 8:00PM at home. The officer told me that a lady was trying to report her husband missing, but it had not been twenty-four hours. Ms. Taylor produced my business card, so the officer called me. Ms. Taylor said that her husband just never came home after going to the grocery store."

"Taylor had LoJack on the car, and it was found by Reagan Airport Authority Police. The CAT is processing it, and Calhoun is at the airport with them. Harrison is at Taylor's house to see if he can develop any leads."

"It was difficult for us to keep McDowell under twenty-four-hour protective custody. The dioceses would not permit us in the church or the rectory with guns. When the other clergy went to check on him after he missed breakfast, they called 9-1-1. His bed doesn't appear to have been slept in. Jefferson went to the church."

Joe caught Wood up on the information that he and Tyler obtained in Valley Cove.

"Joe, we are sure that the numbers are related to the people on the list. They have been found at every murder scene. The stick figure on the mirror appears to be a praying mantis. We aren't sure about the connection. The unsub is a female, and the sketches are all close, with slight changes in each one. Reggie looked at the video and determined that the woman in the bar, the one who went to Logan's room that night, and the woman in the Richmond tape from the bank are one and the same. Reggie explained that people can change their appearance with disguises, but people don't think about altering their gait or stride. He measured the stride in each of the videos and noticed the same patterns of a bounce with the walk. Reggie estimated her to be between five foot eight inches and five foot ten inches tall. He also pointed out the cocktail dress gloves she had on as high-end maybe Sacs or Fredrick's," explained Wood.

"If you two want to go home and get some rest, I will keep you advised, he added." "Joe your friend from the news paper has been snooping around again. We put a lid on him for now; he's not breaking any laws."

"Wood you're doing a good job. Call me or Tyler if something comes up."

Garbesi dropped off Liv and went home to his nice two-story house in Arlington at the rear of the cul-de-sac. He'd lived there for several years and had nice quiet neighbors. The van with the news reporter was sitting on Garbesi's street. When Joe got home, he called the desk sergeant at Arlington PD and asked for a cruiser to chase the pest away. He left his badge, handcuffs, and gun on the kitchen counter got something to eat and went to take a nap. When he awoke, it was dark outside. He checked his cell and home phone; no messages. He called Tyler and then Wood; no new information.

Joe looked out the window. The van wasn't there, and he noticed the dome light was on in his car. He thought that maybe he'd accidently turned it on when he'd turned the head lights off. *I hope the battery isn't dead.* He threw a bathrobe on and grabbed his car keys. He left the door open and went to the car.

When he got to the car, he unlocked the door and felt something like a bee sting hit his neck. He reached up and felt a dart in his neck as darkness set in on him a shadowy figure emerged from behind the garage. The figure caught him before he fell to the ground and rolled him in the back seat of the vehicle. She pushed the rest of his body into the back seat, tied his hands, and gagged him. She popped the trunk and took a blanket out to cover him up. She then ducked behind the garage and retrieved a fold-up bike and placed it in the trunk. She turned off the car dome and took his keys. Carla went to lock up the house and collect a few souvenirs. She entered the house, closing the door behind her. She did not plan on being in there long. She didn't want to call any attention to an open door. She first looked around and noticed a picture of the girl at the diner, and probably her mother. Doenay was the girl's name. She picked up the badge, handcuffs, and gun, and turned all the lights except the living room light off. She'd learned from watching his house that Garbesi always left that light burning.

Carla drove Garbesi's car out I-66 west towards Loudon County Virginia. She pulled off an exit towards Route 17 south. Three miles down Route 17, she turned left onto a gravel road. A quarter mile down the road was a steel-gated locked fence and a sign "NO Trespassing" "Tri County Quarry Properties Hours of Operation; Mon-Fri 8:00AM until 6:00PM." Carla had found this isolated area on Thursday while riding around looking for somewhere to bring McDowell, and Taylor in case the first place she'd found had too much heat. She'd decided it was too far out to transfer two bodies, alive or dead. She figured that Garbesi and his crew were getting too close and this would keep him out of the way, giving her time to finish what she'd started and to disappear. She pulled into an old quarry house, which looked as if it hadn't been used in years.

Carla went inside the shack for a few minutes through the door with the broken locks. She came out and passed smelling salts under Garbesi's nose. Carla said, "Come on Colombo" making reference to a tenacious TV detective of the 1970s. Colombo never gave up until he got his perpetrator.

Joe was still drowsy from the drug Carla had injected him with but could see his weapon pointed in his direction. Carla pointed him toward a basement in the shack, where he could see the faint glow of incandescent lights. When Garbesi got to the basement, she handcuffed one of his wrists to a pipe and then cut the bonds on his hands and removed his gag. "You can scream, no one will hear you. Everyone is gone until Monday morning."

Joe asked; "Are you going to kill me too Darla?"

She glared at him. "Darla has been dead for years. You haven't done anything to me, and you don't deserve to pay for any sins. You just need to be out of the way for a couple days while I finish my quest."

"What would you prefer I call you?" asked Garbesi.

"Call me Belinda, please," she said in a calmer voice. Lieutenant, I want to tell you a story that started back when Darla was about fifteen years old. I know that McDowell explained most of the story, but I need for you to know the rest of it. Darla's stepbrother Clay Jr., sold her body to the highest bidder, actually all bidders. When the stepfather, Clay Senior found out he took the money and beat the hell out of Junior breaking his arm."

"He never let Darla report the crime; however, Darla and her mom tried to, which caused allot of problems for them. Clay Sr. and the sheriff brushed everything under the carpet. You see, those boys didn't only rape Darla. They, ejaculated in her mouth, fucked her in the ass, smeared come all over her, and totally degraded her person."

"She became pregnant, and her stepfather aborted the baby by making her jump from the bed until she miscarried."

"Clay Sr. saw that Junior had come up with a money-generating plan. Junior thought he should get a cut of the proceeds for coming up with the plan. That is when the younger Clay went missing. He and his daddy went out one night, and only Senior came back. Clay Sr. said the boy ran away. Mason Hancock came to see Clay Sr. and went missing too; Junior and Mason are probably at the bottom of a coal mine shaft."

"Darla killed Clay Sr., when he decided to sample the goods before he pimped the two daughters and the step-daughter out."

Garbesi had taken enough psych classes to notice that Darla or Belinda or whatever she wanted to be called was delusional. She kept referring to herself in the third person.

She continued, "Darla was not found guilty but she was sent to a mental institution for evaluation and treatment. Did you know, Joe that not everyone in those places is crazy? Some people have been sent there to shelter them from real prosecution. Darla met Morgan Roane, a rich kid who had a fascination with fire. Morgan actually burned the barn on her daddy's farm down. Daddy didn't want her to go to jail, so he had her committed. She wasn't insane. Darla wasn't insane. She needed to be protected from outside forces."

"Morgan's mother was visiting and took a liking to Darla. The private teacher who came in for Morgan also taught Darla. Darla and Morgan also shared Jose, the security guard. Morgan willingly and Darla being violated twice a week, that bastard shaved off all his hair and used a condom. Darla finally gave in and stopped fighting it. I don't think Morgan knew at first and Darla didn't want to upset her only friend."

"When Darla turned eighteen, she was moved from the child's ward to the adult ward. The problem for Jose now was that Morgan and Darla had rooms close to each other. The administrator knew that Darla did not have a mental problem but wouldn't say she was able to become a productive member of society. The administrator had her working in the office and was flirting with her. He would touch her butt or brush against her breast, making it appear to be an accident. The administrator's name was Herbert Blanchard, about fifty years old and a fairly handsome man."

"One day Darla was roaming around the east wing, which had been being renovated for years. She saw a light on at the end of the hall and walked toward it. She never knew that a room existed in this place that was furnished like an apartment. It must be kept up for one of the big shot visitors, whom periodically checked on the institution, or Blanchard's girl friends. The room had a computer, a full kitchen, shelves full of books on every subject imaginable, and a TV with cable. The TV was on, but no one was inside the room."

"Darla walked into the room and stared at the TV. She was startled by a voice behind her. 'Dear girl, May, I help you?' Darla turned to run but the old lady asked her not to leave; 'I don't get many visitors down here anymore. I live here my name is Helen Pennyloper.'

"Ms. Pennyloper had killed her husband when she caught him cheating. Her husband's family had put her in that place to avoid the embarrassment of a trial, forty years earlier. Helen's families on both sides were big in the banking business. She had thought that they probably forgot her, but they kept sending the big checks to keep her comfortable and for a tax deduction."

"Helen had enough pull with the staff to have Darla come to her room twice a week under the guise of cleaning up. Helen taught Darla to speak four languages, how to use a computer, how to manipulate bank accounts, and how to act like a lady. She also told Darla that, in this world, she needed to learn to use her sexuality to further herself. Helen seemed to have adopted Darla."

"One day, Darla looked out the window in Helen's room and saw a praying mantis. The male was strumming his legs as to entice the female into mating. The smaller bug mounted the larger one.

The female mantis turned around and bit his head off while he was still on top. I guess Darla is doing the same thing. She is hypnotizing these men for sex and then neutralizing or neutering them. Maybe it is payback for taking what was hers and stealing her life."

She paused for a minute; "Where are my manners? Joe, there is water in that camel pack above you." She drank out of it first to show him it was not poison and then wiped the mouth piece with an alcohol wipe.

She continued, "Darla saw that her sex could be the asset that she needed to get out of the place. She took advantage of the administrator's flirting advances by giving him blow- jobs two times a week that curled his toes and fucking him once a week. She acted as if she enjoyed every minute of it. Darla, Morgan and Morgan's mom came up with a plan for the girls to escape and make it look as if they'd both died in the fire. They needed, Jose since the rooms were still locked at night. Morgan's mom was going to leave them one hundred thousand dollars at a designated area."

"Garbesi, I hope I am not putting you to sleep. Do you want to hear about the plan? You aren't going anywhere, and I don't think you'll get to read Darla's diary. We have sometime to kill before I meet Taylor and McDowell. I'll tell you."

Joe spoke up, trying to humor her. "Darla doesn't need to do this we can get her help?"

"Sure, Joe, send her back in the nut hut, or have The Commonwealth of Virginia fry her in the chair or juice her up with go-to-sleep drugs." She calmed down, "Joe, let me continue with my story. Darla and Morgan set the day of the escape with only one minor problem. They wanted to remove all the records the hospital had on their lives in case the fire didn't destroy everything."

"Darla told Morgan about the romps with the administrator. Morgan suggested a threesome, where one of the girls would lift his keys during the distractions. When Darla asked the administrator about it, he was ecstatic. The plan started to gel. Jose got us a small video camera and set it up in the admin office. He showed Darla how it worked and set it for motion detection and a two-hour record time. The administrator gave his wife some bullshit excuse that he had to work late and told the guards he did not want to be disturbed for at least an hour or two. He had to meet a deadline. Darla and Morgan had decided before they went to his office that they were going to enjoy themselves. If they gave the son of bitch a heart attack so what. One thing for certain he would not miss his keys until it was too late. He wouldn't even think of his keys after they laid the smack down pussy on him."

"Morgan and Darla were ushered up the back stairs to a private entrance to his office out of range, of any cameras in the front halls. He must have stopped at a store because he had matching panty sets for the girls, one in yellow the other in red. He pointed them to the shower off to the side of his office. He had them shower together as he stripped to his underwear set in a chair and rubbed his dick. He then instructed them to put on the matching panties and bras, the yellow for Darla and the red for Morgan. The girls looked hot."

"He led them out to the folding couch bed in his office. He needed to rest after a long day sometimes before he went home, he explained. Darla started tongue kissing him and rubbing his chest. He played with her plump, grapefruit size tits, and took off her top. While he was sucking her ample breast, Morgan was busy pulling off his underwear and rubbing his wrinkled cock between her firm boobs to make it rise to the occasion. He was busy nibbling on the rich brown halos surrounding Darla's nipples. When Morgan merged his balls into her mouth and caressed his asshole with her fingers, he let out a low whimper of pleasure."

"The girls were getting hot for each other, but they knew they had to put him into complete euphoria to continue with their plan. Darla kissed down his stomach until she kissed Morgan with a peck and winked at her. Darla took the head of his dick in her mouth and let her tongue dance on the tip of its head. Louder moans of pleasure came from the man, as Morgan moved to his mouth and started rubbing her titties on his face. Darla took his shaft into her mouth and created a suction that even no known vacuum cleaner could match as she withdrew slowly, jacking off his peter as she moved up and down the rod. Darla knew he was ready to explode."

"She and Morgan stopped at the same time. Not so fast. We need to get our nut, too big boy, the girls said in unison."

"His fucked up smile said 'you're right.'

"Morgan set on his hips, driving his dick deep within her recesses, and Darla mounted his face so that she was sitting and looking at Morgan. Darla and Morgan started by French kissing and playing with each others areolas, while he was suckling on Darla's clit and driving his pole into Morgan's cunt. The girls then reversed their seats and he was lapping Morgan's pussy and stuck his package into Darla's box. Morgan started to suck on Darla's, flawless, Gerber-shaped nipples."

"Morgan told him after a few minutes, 'I want you to give it to me doggy style while I am licking Darla's pussy.'

"Darla had never had another woman, but she liked it. The girls had multiple orgasms but still had to focus on the prize of freedom. Darla got Morgan to sit on her face. The administrator fucked Morgan in the mouth, driving his dick into her face up to the hilt."

"The girls decided it was time to let him have his nut. They gave him the option of whom he wanted to come inside. Darla took the rubber off his desk and slid it onto his throbbing red member which looked as if it would blow like a volcano at anytime. Morgan straddled his hips and started the bucking bronco ride. Morgan said she knew it was the end when she used her kegel muscles on him. Darla rubbed Morgan's tits, and he and Morgan finally exploded in shuttering convulsions."

"When he completed Darla took the condom off his flaccid penis and told him, she was going to flush it. He heard the toilet flush. He went into the bathroom, washed off and came back in and lied down. 'Girls, go wash up,' he said. The girls followed instructions."

"When they came back into the room, he was sound asleep. Darla grabbed the keys from his pockets and the video of their sexcapades. The girls cleaned up the room and went down the private stairs. The girls heard the phone ring, and in the office and Blanchard answered. 'Hello, Yes honey. I must have fallen asleep. I'll be home in an hour. Love you too.'

"The girl's went back to their rooms, while Jose watched for the administrator to leave. He let Darla and Morgan out of their rooms. The plan was for Darla to go back to the office, grab all their records, and burn the rest of the files. Meanwhile Morgan and Jose were dousing the boiler room with flammable fuels. They were looking for total incineration of the building, but there would be enough time to evacuate the patients."

"When Darla got back to the basement something, had happened Morgan and Jose were both lying in pools of blood. Jose was dead. Apparently, he'd had a gun and had plans to take out the girls after he'd got the money. Morgan had found out about his plan, or conjectured it, when the weapon had fallen out of his pants while they were running to the boiler room. She'd hit him with a pipe in the head. Jose had then turned and stabbed, then shot her. The noise must have been drowned out by the machinery. Morgan was still alive, but barely, when Darla found her. She told Darla everything, including the stash location before she died."

"Darla doused the bodies with accelerant to burn faster and hotter and to buy herself time. Darla sent a package to the West Virginia States Attorney General detailing the bull-shit that went on at the institution, which included the sex tape and condom. She heard that Blanchard committed suicide, and several other hospital employees were convicted."

"Darla went to get the money and then to see Morgan's mom. Ms. Roane had a stroke and could understand but couldn't respond to what had happened. Darla then went to see her mom and sisters. The family did not know Darla was in Valley Cove. Darla did go to the house and got the list of thirteen, which she had taken from her stepbrother's hiding place after he disappeared."

"Darla went to a small town in Illinois where no one knew her, changed her name, and became a teacher. You might be surprised; with a little money, you can buy a degree and references. Ms. Pennyloper taught Darla well enough that she did not have a hard time convincing a small school system that needed teachers of her credentials. Everything was going well, and Darla, under her new identity established a reputation as a proficient educator who cared about her students. Darla was enjoying a new life for the first time in a long time.

"One afternoon, during a parent-teacher's day a student's father recognized Darla. It was Kevin Gram, one of the shitheads from the list. He couldn't leave well enough alone. Gram must have decided he still wanted some more of Darla's pussy. He found out where Darla lived and decided to visit her that night."

"He was found in a municipal dump a few months later missing his balls. Darla had moved on and decided that, to obtain any peace in life. She needed to delete the list from humanity. Darla said that she was looking for atonement from her assailants."

"Joe, I need to leave to make my meeting. Don't worry, I will call your precinct Monday and tell them where to find you."

Darla picked up Joe's gun from the table, released the ammunition magazine, and pulled the slide to eject the round in the chamber. She took Garbesi's badge, along with the bullets, and put them in her attaché case. "I need a souvenir."

Darla took the bike out of the trunk and ditched Garbesi's car behind the shack in the woods. She rode the bike to the nearest Sheetz gas station, ditched it, and called a cab. The cab took her to the nearest metro station. She retrieved the rental car from the place in DC where she was staying and was on her way.

CHAPTER 13: THE HOUSE

McDowell woke up, in a dusky dirty, basement chained to a wall. The only light was a lantern on a table across the room. Next to him was another man and in the corner was a woman. She appeared to be sleeping.

The second man started to move, "Where am I?"

McDowell spoke, "Ritchie is that you?"

"Who are you responds the prisoner?"

"It's Berkley McDowell don't you remember me."

Taylor asked, "Why did you bring me here?"

"I didn't, I'm being held prisoner too." McDowell said "I think Darla brought us here."

"Who is that in the corner?" asked Ritchie.'

McDowell said "I don't know, but I think she's dead. She hasn't moved in the last twenty minutes."

The door at the top of the stairs opened, and a silhouetted figure with a flashlight came down the steps. "McDowell and Taylor it has been a very long time."

The men spoke together, "Who are you?"

"Well boys, I guess you don't remember me with my clothes on." She came closer, "What's wrong? You look as if you seen a ghost."

McDowell swallowed hard, "You look great Darla!"

Taylor spoke, "Darla Knapper, "You crazy fucking bitch let us go."

"Ritchie don't curse in front of the clergy. I know your mother taught you better."

Taylor started to scream for help.

"Ritchie scream as much as you want. No one can hear you down in this abandoned house. This house has been condemned and is fenced off from the street. I hope you two have had good lives because mine was totally destroyed thanks to both of you."

Taylor spoke first; "Neither of us touched your stinking cunt, you gutter slut whore."

"Ritchie, I am going to have to gag you if you can not tone your language down."

McDowell cleared his throat. "Darla, we were wrong, although we did not violate your body. We didn't come forward when you reported the crime."

Darla glared in contempt at the two men. "You came back that night and covered me, McDowell didn't you? You two had an attack of conscience or didn't want to follow the mess that was spread all over me. Nonetheless you are the last two of the thirteen bastards."

McDowell asked, "Darla, who is she?" He motioned towards the female body on the floor with his head.

"I did not know that someone had claimed this property for themselves. She thought I was a claim jumper. That was unfortunate. When she attacked me, I pushed her and she hit her head. Say a prayer for her, and yourself, McDowell.

"You are a fucking asshole, let us go," screamed Taylor.

Darla grabbed Taylor in the crotch and started to squeeze hard. "I told you Ritchie to show some respect. Now, I'm going to have to gag you."

She tied a gag around Ritchie's mouth while the father said a few words in prayer for all those living and dead in the room.

"Father, that was very nice, but it isn't going to save your lives." Darla started to spread gasoline on the floor of the basement and sprinkled it all over the men. She pulled the corpse over to the middle of the floor and put a set of her clothes including her panties and bra on it. Darla dragged the body under the stairs, positioned it, and then soaked the clothes and exposed skin with gas. Darla walked to the table and put the father's cross and Taylor's wedding ring in the fire proof pouch. She placed the pouch near the body under the steps.

Darla took the Coleman lantern and started up the steps. She stopped and stamped on one step until it cracked and broke. She stepped over the hole, turned around, and struck two road flare. The first one was thrown on the floor between Taylor and McDowell. She dropped the second through the hole in the stair case and onto the stranger's body. She let the lantern fall and bounce, down the steps into the basement, when Darla reached the door at the top of the stairs

CHAPTER 14:
THE WRAP

Wood and Tyler found Garbesi on Sunday night. Joe was a little stiff but was cleared by the medics.

Joe asked, "Did Darla call you?"

Liv answered, "No, your friend in the van from the newspaper was sitting on a street close to your neighborhood. PD got a call, and the patrol officers remembered a call from the previous night on the same vehicle. When patrol went to check it out, they found the driver unconscious in the rear of the van. All he could remember was an attractive woman asking him for help because her car broke down, and everything else was a blank. The desk sergeant told the patrol to check on your house. Your car was gone. When Wood tried your cell phone there was no answer. You never answer, though."

Liv continued, "We noticed the receiver in the van. Our friend had put a tracking device on your car, and it kept blinking on the scope in the van, as if it wasn't moving. We tracked your car to this location."

Liv asked, "Did she touch anything in the shack."

"She had on black cocktail gloves that went to her elbows." Joe thought for a minute.

"She drank from the camel pack and wiped off the tube but there may be some DNA inside the tube."

Wood spoke up, "McDowell, Taylor and Roane all appear to be dead. They burned up in a fire early this morning in an abandon property in Arlington. We don't have confirmation yet but preliminary reports believe it is them. We will know more on Monday. The bodies have been moved to La Net's office. The forensics team and fire marshals are in the house now."

Tyler said, "We won't know anything until Monday. Lieutenant, you need to get some rest. We all need some rest. We can start sorting this out in the morning."

Garbesi nodded in agreement, "tomorrow early."

Monday morning, La Net called and asked Joe and Liv to come to the coroner's office. Dr. Fayette met them at the door and led them to the autopsy room. "The men are confirmed to be McDowell and Taylor from dental records. A liquid fuel was poured on their bodies. They were burned alive. The lungs on both victims were full of smoke. The female has not been identified yet. She was most likely dead before the fire, and no smoke was present in her lungs. Her body was also doused in fuel. She had blunt force trauma to her head. It may have happened when the stairs gave away. The gas can was close to the body. I don't know if we can get dentals on her. It appeared as if she had a flare or something that burned very hot land near her face, hot enough to totally incinerate the jaw."

The detectives went back to the office after meeting with the coroner.

Back at the office, Wood had information to share with Joe and Liv. "The CAT found a fire proof pouch close to the female casualty with souvenirs from all the murder victims and your badge Lieutenant. A diary detailing each of the murders and the story you said your captor told when you were her prisoner was also located in the bag. There were blood smears on some of the pages, which appear to be from a paper cut. They have been swabbed and sent to the lab for screening and typing."

Joe said, "Everyone involved in this case in the conference room."

When everyone was in the conference and seated, Garbesi addressed the detectives. "The case isn't closed yet, not until we get a positive identification. Keep working it as if it were still active. Calhoun, have Harrison help you track down anyone in the diary we didn't know about. Liv see if you can match the souvenir property to owner's or relatives of owners. Wood said, a rental car was found about two blocks from the fire and patrol believes that our subject rented it. The CAT is processing."

He added, "I don't think the body belongs to Darla. Jefferson, check the airlines for the last two days for Roane, Hardy, or Knapper. We don't know what name she is using this time."

Liv waited until the other detectives had left the room and then spoke up, "Joe there were seventeen passports and matching driver's licenses, including Roane and Hardy's in the bag. We have other cases pending. Do you think we should devote all our resources to this case?"

"Humor me," Liv, "She could have killed me at any time but she didn't. She is a very clever woman."

EPILOGUE

It was Christmas time in the Washington, DC, area. A little chill was in the air, but no snow. The mail had been dropped on Garbesi's desk.

Sgt. Tyler poked her head into Garbesi's office. "Joe the chief wants us to close the Logan/Knapper case. Every jurisdiction involved, even those that listed victims as missing and then reclassified them as homicides, has except for us. There hasn't been another murder since the fire three months ago. The fireproof bag that was recovered had a wealth of evidence, leading every agency involved to believe that it was Darla Knapper who committed the murders. The handwriting samples from the bank check, the school in Illinois and the diary at the fire scene conclusively pointed to her. Darla's jewelry was even in the bag. I don't think she would have left that behind. We have a DNA profile from the blood in the journal matched to DNA that was recovered from the house and clothes that the charred body was wearing. The money was never recovered, but that is the FBI's problem. Relatives are waiting to receive the property of their loved ones and have been calling the chief daily."

She handed Joe the paper work to sign off.

"You know Liv I don't believe Darla is dead but I will sign off." Garbesi signed the papers closing the case.

"We can always reopen the case if we have new evidence," said Liv.

"Liv how often does that happen?" Joe queried.

"Liv, what are you doing for the holidays."

"Holmes has invited me to Valley Cove for the holidays." Liv replied. "I am going to return the property to those folks who lost relatives, including Darla's jewelry to her sister. I looked at my life and it has been all work and no play. I am going to enjoy myself. What about you Joe?"

"Darla made me think. She lost her father when she was young. Holmes was a role model for her until her stepfather messed it up. She might have turned out different. I need to go see my daughter and try to develop a relationship. I hope she accepts me."

"I think Doenay will accept you Joe." Liv looked at him a woman knows these things. You don't need to talk about them. I am sure that Doenay knows or suspects too."

Joe locked his office without looking at the mail. A postcard from Aruba was sitting in the middle of the stack it read. "I wish we would have met under different circumstances. It is beautiful here. With Love." There was no signature.

Joe past the break room as he was leaving to wish the detectives a Merry Christmas. The local news was on.

The female news reporter said "In a note of generosity and Christmas spirit, an anonymous donor gave twenty-five million dollars to the Society for Victims of Rape, twenty-five million dollars for Child and Spouse Abuse Victims and twenty-five million dollars to Education and Child Development".

That leaves her more then twenty-four million to play with, Joe thought to himself.